RAND'S REDEMPTION

BY
KAREN VAN DER ZEE

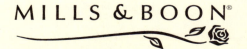

MILLS & BOON®

*First published in Great Britain 2001
Harlequin Mills & Boon Limited,
Eton House, 18-24 Paradise Road, Richmond, Surrey TW9 1SR*

© Karen van der Zee 2001

ISBN 0 263 17083 7

*Set in Times Roman 10¼ on 11½ pt.
07-0901-50320*

*Printed and bound in Great Britain
by Antony Rowe Ltd, Chippenham, Wiltshire*

"What I want is you. I want you. I want you in my bed."

Shanna's heart leaped to her throat. "Why does that scare you?" she whispered, tilting her head back so she could see his face.

"Because I don't know how simple this is...or will be." Rand paused. "And I don't want you to get hurt in the end."

"If I get hurt, I'll take responsibility for it," she said. "I am here with you out of my own free will. I can leave any time I don't want to be with you anymore."

"You sound so brave," he said quietly.

She felt relief at his smile. She smiled back. "You have no idea how brave."

Ever since **Karen van der Zee** was a child growing up in Holland she wanted to do two things: write books and travel. She's been very lucky. Her American husband's work as a development economist has taken them to many exotic locations. They were married in Kenya, had their first daughter in Ghana and their second in the United States. They spent two fascinating years in Indonesia. Since then they've added a son to the family as well, and lived for a number of years in Virginia before going on the move again. After spending over a year in the West Bank near Jerusalem, they are now living again in Ghana, but not for good!

CHAPTER ONE

SHANNA noticed the man from quite a distance as he came striding down the busy street toward the Thorn Tree Café terrace. It was hard not to. Amid the colorful crowd of tourists sporting cameras, men in business suits, Indian women in exotic saris and Arabs in flowing robes, he looked tall and casual in his khaki slacks and short-sleeved shirt. He had long legs and he moved with the grace of an athlete. Or an animal, free and proud in the wild.

He entered the terrace where she was sitting with Nick and glanced around. His dark hair was curly and cropped close, his blue eyes clear and sharp.

He was coming toward them.

Her stomach tightened, her pulse quickened and she felt a delicious thrill of excitement—a different kind of excitement than she had felt ever since she'd woozily stumbled off the plane in Nairobi last night—a kind of excitement that made you think of romantic music and starry nights, the kind that made your heart do dance steps.

Barely off the plane and she was dreaming already. Well, why not. Today was a golden day.

A day full of exotic sights and tropical sunshine and bright promise. A day full of secret anticipation of what was to come. She was finally back in the place where she had spent the four happiest years of her life as a girl. Oh, how long she had dreamed of this!

She felt Nick's arm around her shoulder. He smiled at her. "It's good to see you happy," he said. "Keep it up okay?"

She was touched by the warmth in his eyes. She rubbed

5

her cheek against his shoulder. "I'll be fine, Nick. A change of scenery will do me good, something to occupy my mind."

He tightened his arm around her, kissed her cheek. "Good, then I'm glad you came."

And then he was there, the stranger, looming in front of them.

Nick leaped to his feet with a wide grin and the men shook hands. The man was taller than Nick, who was tall by anyone's standard. He looked like he belonged on a movie screen—confident, self-assured. As if he owned the world.

Well, he owned part of it.

Seventy-five thousand acres of hills and jungle and savannah in the Rift Valley, where he raised sheep and cattle and lived in a big, gorgeous house on the edge of a cliff. Just like in the movies. She'd seen the pictures Nick had taken some years ago, and last year a magazine had featured an article on the ranch and the research work conducted there by the Kenyan government and the African Wildlife Organisation. Looking at the man, she could easily imagine him in a Land Rover or on a horse, or flying a little Cessna, all of which he probably did.

Nick turned to face her with a smile. "Shanna, this is Rand Caldwell. Rand, Shanna Moore, my niece."

She extended her hand and he took it in his huge hard one. For a pregnant moment he said nothing, just stared at her with his penetrating blue gaze. In the tanned face his eyes looked impossibly light, and disturbingly icy.

"Miss Moore," he said in cool British tones, and released her hand.

Meeting new people was not usually a source of apprehension for her. However, this man made her feel off balance. Why was he looking at her like this?

"Nice to meet you," she said, and offered him her cheeriest smile, trying not to show him he'd unnerved her, which he had. "Nick told me all about your ranch."

Rand lifted a quizzical brow and glanced over at Nick. "You haven't seen it in years," he said dryly.

Nick grinned. "It made an indelible impression. Especially that lioness that nearly tore me apart."

Nick was, biologically, her uncle, but in reality he was more like a big brother. He was a fun-loving guy with a sense of the adventurous, eleven years older than she. Since the death of her parents six years ago, it was at Nick and his wife Melanie's home she'd spent Christmas and other holidays. They were her family now.

"How's Melanie?" Rand asked.

"Very well," said Nick. "Busy with the children. She's sorry she couldn't come along." In his student days Rand had spent a couple of years studying in the States and had become friends with Melanie and Nick.

The men ordered beer and Shanna asked for another passion fruit juice, nectar of the gods. She listened absently to the conversation, sipping her juice and watching the colorful melee of humanity pass by in the busy street.

A tall blond woman maneuvered her way through the maze of chairs and tables, a baby in her arms, his little face blissfully asleep on her shoulder.

Sammy.

A rush of longing. Instant, fierce. She could feel the weight of his small body in her arms, smell his sweet baby smell. Tears burned behind her eyes. She glanced down at her lap, pressed her eyes closed and took a deep, steadying breath.

Sammy was all right. She had to believe that. She took another deep breath.

Think of something else, she told herself.

Like Rand Caldwell and his icy eyes.

Focusing on the men's voices, she heard them talk about

politics and her thoughts drifted to the ranch, the pictures she had seen.

The ranch, she knew, was only twenty miles from Kanguli, the village where she had lived with her parents as a child. What she wanted to do more than anything else was to run out into the street, hijack the first Jeep or Land Rover passing by and drive out to Kanguli right this minute. Unfortunately she'd have to wait till tomorrow, when she'd pick up her own rented Land Rover. She hoped she could still find the village. Would the people still remember her after all this time?

She watched Rand as he talked. He had a somewhat prominent nose, a square chin, a high forehead—a face like a living sculpture, angular and masculine. And those piercing eyes…

She glanced down at his hands holding his beer glass. They were big and brown and strong. Capable, competent hands. It would be interesting to see him in action on the ranch.

He looked at her suddenly, as if he realized that she'd been studying him. For a moment their eyes locked. The cool disdain in his face was unsettling. Why was he looking at her like that?

She heard Nick talking about her, telling Rand that she was writing an article for a university publication.

"And you're here to do research?" Rand asked politely.

"Yes," she said. This was partially the truth, if not the whole truth.

"And you happened to come out at the same time as Nick?" he asked levelly.

She nodded. "My schedule was flexible, so I made it fit his."

"And what are you going to write about?" His tone indicated he couldn't care less.

"I'm doing a piece on Kenyan women, how their lives

have changed in the last generation, their position in the family, the society and the workforce.''

One dark brow cocked. ''Really?'' His voice was heavy with sarcasm.

She groaned inwardly, knowing full well what he was thinking. He thought she was here for two weeks. The idea of writing a well-researched article of that nature in two weeks, being fresh in a foreign country, was laughable.

Only, she wasn't a stranger to the country, and she wasn't staying for two weeks—not if her plans worked out, and she was determined that they should. However, she could not set Mr. Rand Caldwell straight because Nick didn't know about her intentions yet. She didn't want to worry him.

Rand was looking at her, narrow-eyed, contemplating no doubt if she were merely acting like a fool, or, in actual fact, was one.

Nick patted her hand and drew his tall body out of the chair. ''I need to make a phone call. Can I trust you two alone for a few minutes?''

Shanna rolled her eyes at him and he grinned.

Left alone with Rand, Shanna was well aware of a certain disconcerting electricity in the air between them. For a reason she couldn't begin to understand, this man did not like her. Perhaps it was best to simply ignore the vibes he was sending out and pretend she had no idea. Well, she didn't. At least not *why* he seemed to be so chilly toward her.

''I understand there is a lot of wild game on your property,'' she said, ''and you're very involved in conservation.''

He took a swallow of beer. ''Yes.'' His voice was curt and impatient.

''I saw the article they did on your work at the ranch last year,'' she went on. ''Why did you decide to allow your place to be used for research?''

''Because I think it is important,'' he said, as if he were talking to a dim-witted child. She let it pass, trying to remember what else had been in the article. It had mentioned the house which was built on the edge of a wild and rocky gorge. Magnificent views, dramatic scenery, the report had said, and the photos had been dramatic indeed. She'd love to see the place.

She took a drink from her juice and a thought occurred to her. It was rather a brave thought, she had to admit, but why not take a risk? She had nothing to lose.

"You have a big place," she stated. "Do you have women employees, farm workers?"

"Yes." He reached for his glass.

"I wonder if I could visit some time and talk to the women. If it wouldn't be an inconvenience, of course."

"I doubt it will be helpful," he said with barely restrained condescension.

"I think it might be." She produced a smile. "And of course, if you know other women who would be willing to talk to me, I would appreciate your help."

His eyes narrowed slightly and he was silent for a moment. She had confused him with her appeal. He was emitting hostile vibrations and he had expected to receive the same in return. Instead, she was appealing to his gentleman instincts and asking for help.

He leaned back in his chair, his eyes probing hers. "I'll let you know." His tone of voice indicated that she might as well forget the whole idea.

She smiled. She was determined to stay civil and keep her dignity. "Thank you. It's important I talk to as many different kinds of women as possible to get a balanced impression."

"And you think you can accomplish that in two weeks?"

She shrugged. "I've done extensive research."

"I see," he said in a tone that indicated he doubted it very much.

She pretended not to notice his animosity. The best defense was no defense at all.

They sat in silence, and she watched the people around her.

"Nick told me you were born in Kenya, that you grew up here," she said after a while, making another effort at civilized conversation, "and that the ranch has been in your family since your grandfather came to Kenya from England in the early twenties."

His mouth tightened. "Yes."

She leaned forward in her chair. "I'm sorry, I don't mean to...pry. I'm just trying to make conversation." She smiled again, but it was taking quite an effort.

"Naturally." He radiated cold dislike.

It was amazing. What was the matter with this man? She hadn't asked anything that wasn't printed in the article. She leaned back in her chair and decided to get away from the personal.

"It's wonderful to be here. I'm looking forward to the party tonight, meeting people."

She was quite comfortable with her own company, but now and again she enjoyed parties and other get-togethers where she had the opportunity to meet interesting people, learn new things.

He did not respond, but then of course she had not asked a question; she'd merely made a comment, and he certainly didn't seem inclined to make an effort to keep the conversation going. Perhaps, living alone, he had forgotten how to talk and be sociable.

"Living in such an isolated place must get lonely at times," she commented. "What do you do for entertainment?"

"Entertainment is not high on my list of priorities. I have a ranch to run."

And certainly he had no time for anything as frivolous as

entertainment, came the automatic thought. "Yes, of course," she said evenly, "but a person can't always work. A modest dose of fun now and then is good for the soul."

He took a swallow of beer and said nothing.

"If you have one," she added, unable to help herself.

He raised his brows in mild derision, still saying nothing and she was tempted to pour her drink over his handsome head but managed to contain herself.

"Do you?" she asked. "Have a soul?"

"I doubt it," he said, and there was the merest quiver of his mouth, but she might have imagined it. She wondered what made him smile, laugh. What made him happy.

"What do you enjoy most about your work? What is it that gives you pleasure?"

He raised his brows. "You certainly seem to be preoccupied with fun and joy and pleasure," he said, his voice sounding as if these were unsavory pastimes no moral person should get involved with.

"Not to mention happiness," she added, smiling sweetly. "I enjoy my work, I enjoy my friends. I like being happy, and if I may be so blunt, there seems to be a great lack of all that in your disposition." She came to her feet. "Excuse me, I think my hair needs combing."

Rand watched her go. Lovely legs, sexy body. She was beautiful, with her blond hair and green eyes and that gorgeous sunny smile. An empty-headed party girl, no doubt. His stomach clenched painfully.

Blond hair and green eyes.

An image floated through his mind, the face of another woman, smiling. The scent of violets. He thought of the twelve-year-old boy lying in bed, trying desperately not to cry because men don't cry. He thought of promises made and never kept. He squashed the memories forcefully, swallowing the bitter taste in his mouth. It had been years since he'd allowed himself to think of her. It was all in the past, done, over with.

Instead, he thought of Melanie, the way he remembered her, long ago, looking at Nick, hopelessly in love. Her happy face, the love in her eyes. So young and naive, so blind.

There was no denying that Nick had been a true friend to him in his college years in the States. There was also no denying that Nick had been an irrepressible skirt chaser, breaking hearts left, right and center. Rand sighed and rubbed his forehead.

He had warned Melanie, but she had not heeded that warning. Instead of running the other way, she had married him. And now here was Nick, far away from home, with this woman, his *niece*.

Shanna was in her hotel room, which adjoined Nick's, and plopped herself down on the big, comfortable bed. It was a gorgeous room, nicely furnished with rattan furniture with cushions upholstered in some bright, tropical fabric, and interesting batik art on the wall.

She stretched out on the bed and let out a deep sigh. She had almost lost her temper with Mr. Rand Caldwell, but not quite.

After she'd returned from the ladies' room, she'd found Nick back at the table and soon after that they'd left to go back to their hotel, and Rand to the house of friends where he was staying.

His supercilious manner was infuriating, not to mention offensive. For some incomprehensible reason, he did not like her. Or was she just imagining it? Was she paranoid? Certainly not. She'd never been paranoid, so why now? Surely it was not a virus one caught on a plane or from drinking alien water.

She yawned, feeling exhausted. She glanced at the bedside clock. She had two hours before they'd have to leave for the party, enough time for a nap. And tomorrow the Great Adventure would begin in earnest.

A thought suddenly occurred to her. Giving a frustrated groan, she slipped off the bed, opened one of the dresser drawers and took out a thick, padded envelope. It was too big to fit in the small safe in her room and she'd intended to put it in the hotel's safe but it had been too late last night. And this morning she'd forgotten to take care of it in her eagerness to start exploring the city.

Slipping back into her shoes, she grabbed her purse and key card and left the room. She stood in the elevator and hugged the envelope to her chest, smiling to herself. She would take no risks. The originals were in her safe-deposit box at her bank in Boston and she'd brought a photo copy as well as a copy on disk to use with her laptop.

Oh, Dad, she said silently, *I'll get it done! I'll make you proud!* Her eyes blurred suddenly and she swallowed hard. She was going to do what she had planned for some time now, and she was going to do it right here in Kenya. Pressing the envelope even tighter against her, she blinked back her tears, feeling an odd mixture of both sadness and joy.

Nick would not be happy when she told him she intended to stay in the country on her own. He felt protective of her, which was nice, but she was twenty-seven and she knew what she wanted and he and Melanie did not need to worry about her anymore. She was going to be fine.

The elevator door opened and she stepped into the massive lobby with its potted palms and crystal chandeliers and exotic artwork. All very comfortable, very luxurious. Tomorrow she would be out driving in the country, see the lush green hills planted with tea and coffee, the flat bush, the tall giraffes, the leaping gazelles. Excitement tickled her blood and she could hardly wait.

After the envelope had been safely tucked away, she went straight back to her room, stripped off her clothes and took a quick shower in the sumptuous bathroom. Draped in a cotton robe provided by the hotel, she collapsed on the bed and fell asleep almost instantly.

It was not a restful slumber. She dreamed that she was back in Kanguli and the house was gone. All the huts were empty and there were no people. She called out for her father but he did not come, and then Rand appeared out of nowhere and stood there looking at her with his cold eyes, saying nothing. It was so awful that she could not stand it and broke into tears. *Don't look at me like that!* she sobbed. *Why are you looking at me like that?* But he merely lifted a sardonic brow and gave no answer. *I want to know where my father is!* she cried. *I have to tell him something!*

Your father is dead, he said, *and you can't stay here. You have no business being here.* And then there was the sound of drums coming from the village and suddenly she was awake.

It wasn't the sound of drums she'd heard, she realized, but Nick knocking on the door connecting their two rooms. "Shanna? Are you awake?"

Shivering, she hugged herself. "Yes, yes, I am." She glanced at the clock on the bedside table. She had forty minutes. "I'll get ready."

She dressed in a simple silk dress of deep cobalt blue. It was slim-fitting and discreetly sexy. As she examined herself in the mirror, the image of Rand flitted through her head and a small shiver of apprehension ran down her back. She shook it away impatiently.

With more vigor than necessary, she brushed out her hair. She was not going to let the man ruin her good time. She intended to enjoy the evening. If he did not like her, it was his problem, not hers.

She left her hair loose, put in long earrings, and stepped into high heels. Straightening her shoulders, she lifted her chin and grinned at her reflection in the mirror. "Go for it, girl,'' she said out loud, and knocked on the connecting door.

Nick was ready to go.

"Stunning," he said and grinned at her.

"Thank you, suh," she drawled and smiled back at him. Secretly she had to admit to herself that she was glad she didn't have to face Rand by herself.

The man in question looked devastatingly handsome in his dark trousers and white jacket and her heart skittered crazily when she saw him enter the hotel lobby just as she and Nick emerged from the elevator. She willed herself to be calm, putting a little zip in her step as they crossed the lobby to meet him. She offered him a sunny smile which found no answer in his implacable face.

His frosty-blue gaze slipped over her from head to toe and he gave a tight little nod in greeting. "Ready?" he asked.

They left the lobby to find his car. It was a dusty Land Rover, a rugged vehicle that looked as if it was not used to an easy life.

"I apologize for the inferior transportation," Rand said, sounding like he didn't give a hoot.

She smiled brightly. "No problem." She wondered if she'd manage to get a smile from him tonight. His face looked like he didn't do a lot of smiling. How could you not smile owning your own piece of paradise in this gorgeous country?

Like a gentleman, he held the door open for her and she slipped in the passenger seat in front. Whatever his attitude, his manners were all there, which was reassuring. Nick got into the back. The interior looked clean enough apart from the dried-up reddish dirt on the floor where muddy boots had tracked it in.

The party was held at a large, beautiful house at the outskirts of Nairobi, the private home of Lynn and Charlie

Comstock, people on the faculty of the university that had invited Nick to do his lectures.

Lynn Comstock was an interesting person of mixed Italian and English descent who had lived all her life in Kenya. She had very dark hair, dancing silvery-gray eyes and a lively face. She asked about Shanna's work, and after several questions turned suddenly around, surveyed the guests and waved Rand over.

"Rand! Shanna's been telling me about an article she's writing about…"

"I know," he said. "She told me."

"You must invite her to your place, let her talk to Wambui! She's perfect! And that old Pokot woman, now there's a character for you!"

"I already asked," Shanna said. "Rand does not think it will be useful for me to talk to anyone there."

Lynn gave him an exasperated look. "Oh, for heaven's sake, Rand!"

He gave her a steely look. "Excuse me, please," he said politely, and strode away. Lynn rolled her eyes and turned away. "The man is impossible," she said to Shanna. "He's taking after his father more and more. Practically lives like a recluse, or at least that's what it seems like. I can't believe he made it to the party."

"Does he have something against women?"

Lynn laughed. "He just doesn't want them too close. Very standoffish." She took a sip of her wine.

"So I've noticed," said Shanna. Maybe it wasn't just her, then. "I just met him this afternoon and he acted as if I'd crawled out of some primordial swamp."

Lynn put her glass down. "He's usually civil enough, in his own inimitable enigmatic fashion. But I find it amazing how the women go for that remote composure of his. They seem to find it intriguing."

"But you don't?"

Lynn laughed. "Hades, no. It annoys me no end. I like my men to be up front. I like to know what I'm dealing with. Well, more or less." She grinned. "You've met my Charlie?"

Shanna had. Charlie was hard to miss with his red beard and exuberant personality. At this moment he was playing the piano and singing Irish drinking songs.

"Women are always after Rand," said Lynn. "Slavering practically. Well, he is one handsome hunk, as they say in America, and having that fancy ranch and all that money doesn't hurt either. "

Shanna could well imagine.

Lynn gave a crooked grin. "The naive idiots. They all think they're the one who'll break through his reserve and discover the passion underneath, but so far I don't believe anyone ever has, not even Marina." She took a fresh drink from a tray passed around by a handsome African waiter in pristine white. "Frankly, I don't think there is any passion. I'm beginning to think he's as unfeeling on the inside as on the outside and that he prefers the company of animals over humans."

"Who's Marina?" Shanna couldn't help herself.

Lynn glanced at Shanna. "She lived with him for over a year. She's a painter, Australian. One day she'd had enough, packed up and left. She stayed with us for a while. She said she'd had enough of living with someone who kept her at an emotional distance all the time." Lynn sighed. "It was sad, really, because I think Marina really loved him." She glanced at her wineglass. "Oh, I never learn," she moaned. "Shoot me, please."

"Learn what?" asked Shanna.

"To keep my mouth shut. Two glasses of wine and I lose all my discretion. All I do is talk and spout out whatever comes to mind." She gave Shanna a pleading look. "I don't mean to be such a gossip, really. I had no business telling you this, although everyone knows anyway, but..." She shrugged, making a face. "Sorry."

The party went on. Shanna was standing with a small group of women, talking, when she noticed Rand nearby. He was observing something intently and the expression on his face made her breath catch in her throat. She stared at him, taking in the faint smile that softened his features, the eyes warm with amusement. Her heart made a leap that almost hurt.

She tore her gaze away and glanced in the direction he was looking and felt her own face warming with a smile. The object of his tender gaze was a little Indian girl, four or five years old, dressed up in a tiny party sari, a bright, shimmering affair shot with gold. Kohl circled her large eyes, blusher faintly colored her cheeks and lipstick brightened her lips. She looked like a delicate costume doll, perfect, beautiful—except for the expression in her dark eyes, which were full of very unladylike mischief.

Shanna had no idea why the little girl was at a grown-up party, but there she was, pretty as an exotic butterfly, fluttering among the adults, cooking up something naughty.

Shanna looked back at Rand, feeling a softening inside her, a strange, ephemeral feeling of elation. And then he met her eyes and his face hardened and all the amusement and warmth vanished from his eyes.

Her stomach lurched and she clenched her hands around her glass and turned away, giving her attention again to the Kenyan woman by her side, a doctor working in a maternity clinic.

Sometime later she found Nick standing next to her. "You're not *working,* by any chance, are you?" he whispered in her ear.

She laughed and hooked her arm through his. "I'm just talking, enjoying myself."

He grinned down at her. "You don't fool me."

"Women everywhere *like* talking about their lives, Nick. All I do is listen." She laughed and then her eyes caught Rand's cold gaze directed at her and her laughter froze. She let go of Nick's arm and took a drink from her glass.

"My, that Rand is a cold one," she said to Nick, and she saw him frown.

"He never was one of the world's great extroverts, but I have to admit I seem to remember him as more congenial." Nick shrugged. "It's been a long time since I saw him last." He studied her with a sudden gleam in his eyes. "Why don't you warm him up a little, Shanna? You're good at loosening people up. Give him some of that irresistible charm of yours."

She grimaced. "I tried. He's immune."

"He keeps looking at you, I've noticed."

"Oh, really? You must be imagining it," she said lightly. But he hadn't, and she knew it.

She was standing at the buffet table surveying the food when Rand appeared next to her.

"You're quite the party girl, aren't you?" he asked, an unmistakable hint of mockery in his voice.

For a moment she just stared at him. Since when was it a sin to be gregarious and happy, to enjoy being with people? Since when did that make you automatically a shallow or frivolous person? Well, apparently in his mind it did.

She resisted the urge to say something sharp in return. He wasn't going to goad her, she was determined. Instead, she gave him a cheery smile.

"I'm enjoying myself. That's all right, isn't it? I mean, there isn't something wrong with having fun, is there?"

His mouth twisted and he reached for some of the food and placed it on his plate without answering her.

She tilted her head and made a show of observing him. "You don't look like you're having any fun. You ought to work on it a little, you know. Live dangerously. Smile a little. You might just like it.'' She couldn't help taunting him; his arrogant attitude was bringing out the worst in her.

He gave her a stony stare. ''I didn't come here to have fun.''

''That's a shame,'' she said, pseudo-sympathetic. ''So, why are you here, then?''

''Business.''

''Oh, I see. Is that why you look so grim? Business is not fun? You don't enjoy your work?''

There was a silence as he observed her with wintry eyes. ''Not everything in life is fun. But if fun is what drives you, let me assure you that I have none to offer you.''

Shanna had had little experience being treated with disdain. Hot indignation welled up inside her. The man was offensive, insufferable and infuriating. It was tempting to tell him so, but presenting him with her opinion of him would only give him satisfaction, she was sure. She managed, with admirable control, to keep her cool and not show him the anger heating her blood. Instead, she nodded solemnly at his statement.

''I figured that one out all by myself,'' she said calmly. ''You're no fun at all.'' She sighed theatrically, she couldn't help herself. ''I'm afraid you're a lost cause.''

''Oh,'' he said lazily, ''perhaps it depends on whose cause. Not all men are fooled by beauty and charm.''

His meaning was clear. She had beauty and charm, but he wasn't fooled by her. The man was an ego maniac. Her stunned mind grasped wildly for an apt reply, failing miserably.

Rand picked up his plate, offering her a contemptuous look. ''Now, if you'll excuse me?''

He strode off, leaving her speechless and seething.

CHAPTER TWO

THREE days later, sitting on a rock in the bush, peering through her binoculars, Shanna was still seething.

She'd been trying very hard not to think about Rand Caldwell. It was not easy. Fortunately, baboons proved a great distraction, infinitely more amusing than the hermit man with the cold eyes. She focused the binoculars on the cliffs in the near distance, zeroing in on a tiny baby baboon clinging to its mother's back, holding on for dear life as she leaped around with the rest of the troop, foraging for food. They were yanking out grasses, digging up roots, peeling fruits. Shanna could not believe she was here, by the cliffs near Kanguli, watching the baboons, as if she had never left.

She had found the village with its thatch-roofed mud huts, found the old house where she'd lived for four years, a dilapidated colonial settlers' house abandoned by its English owners at Independence decades before. She'd seen a line of washing—jeans and T-shirts and brightly colored Jockey undershorts with some intriguing designs. A man lived in the house now, a male with a sense of humor, a Peace Corps or VSO volunteer probably, but no one had been at home yesterday, or today.

And she'd found the baboons. She did not recognize any of the animals, but of course she would not. Too much time had passed. The old ones had died, young ones grown up and new ones born. Also, it might not be the same troop. She ached to come closer, but she knew well enough it was out of the question. They did not know her and it was dangerous.

She was so entranced in watching the baboons' activities,

22

that the sound of a car engine startled her. A Land Rover came bumping over the uneven terrain toward the rocks where she was sitting. She trained the binoculars on the dirt-covered vehicle and saw Rand behind the steering wheel. Her heart turned over and she lowered the binoculars in her lap.

Rand? What was he doing here?

If fun is what drives you, may I assure you that I have none to offer you. His words flashed through her mind, the outrageous insinuation flooding her with new indignation. Her stomach clenched. Why was he here now, disturbing her peace? Sucking in a fortifying breath, she braced herself.

The vehicle came to a stop and Rand leaped out. He wore khaki shorts, a shirt with the sleeves rolled up to the elbows and a battered bush hat. He came toward her with a long-legged stride and as she watched him, her anger whooshed away and all she could do was sit there and look at him, feeling...

She didn't know what she was feeling.

She couldn't help but notice how much he seemed to fit in the rugged landscape—the strength of his body, his hard, powerful features and the sharp eyes that seemed to miss nothing. He was all male and the sense of it stirred the female inside her. There seemed to be nothing she could do about it. Her mouth went dry and she felt a sense of very elemental attraction, a primitive delight in the male beauty of the man coming toward her.

She sat motionless as she watched him approach, aware of nothing but him and the racing of her heart, as if everything else between them had fallen away, had never happened.

"What are you doing here?" she asked, and it came out in a whisper.

"I was looking for you," he said, his voice oddly low, as if it was hard to speak.

I was looking for you.

A simple sentence, yet it seemed imbued with meaning and it filled her head with light.

Sudden wild screams blew in on the wind and the fragile spell shattered, bringing back reality with shocking sharpness. Dragging in air, Shanna whipped her head toward the cliffs and automatically brought the binoculars to her eyes. Her hands were trembling.

One of the male baboons was romancing a female, who was not in the mood and shrieked at him. The male scampered off.

"What was that?" Rand asked, peering into the distance.

She lowered the binoculars and took in another fortifying breath. "A female chasing off a male." The humor hit her as she heard herself say the words and she couldn't help smiling.

His expression gave nothing away. He looped his thumbs behind his belt. "What are you doing here?" he asked, his voice businesslike.

It was as if those magical moments had never happened.

Maybe they had not. Maybe the odd awareness, the strange sensation of recognition had only occurred in her imagination, like a dream. Like a fleeting reflection in crystalline water.

She saw him watching her as she sat there in the grass behind the rocks, her shorts and T-shirt dusty and wrinkled. She'd been here for hours.

"I've been watching the baboons," she said.

His brows shot up, his look incredulous. She could well imagine his surprise. The little scene he was witnessing did not fit the image he had of her—a femme fatale dressed in a sexy dress who used her beauty and charm to seduce men in wicked ways. Here she was sitting in the bush, wearing hiking boots, her hair a tangled mess, watching monkeys.

She gave a half smile. "I like baboons. They're very smart, very human in many ways."

He studied her for a moment, not commenting. "Nick told me you used to live here with your parents."

"Yes, I did. We moved here when I was eleven and we were here for four years. My mother was a teacher and she home-schooled me. I spent hours watching baboons." She'd pretended to be a scientist, like her father, writing her observations in a notebook. Drawing pictures. When she'd learned to recognize the individual animals, distinguish one from the other, she'd give them names—Snoopy, Frisky, Dreamer.

He looked meaningfully at her binoculars. "With the limited time you have at your disposal, I'd have expected you to be working on your writing, not watching baboons."

She felt her hackles rise at his insinuated criticism. She came to her feet, pulled her T-shirt straight and dusted off her shorts. "I spent all day yesterday talking to the women in the village," she said levelly.

They remembered her, of course, the girl with hair the color of maize, and it had been wonderful to see the recognition dawn in their dark eyes, see their smiles, hear their laughter. Suddenly she no longer was a stranger. So they'd sat and talked as they drank many glasses of hot, sweet *chai*—milky, sugary tea. They'd told her of deaths and weddings and births. The girls she had known as a child all had husbands, all had children. They'd wanted to know why she was not yet married, did not have babies.

It had been difficult to explain, so far away from the context of her life at home. Yes, she'd been in love, had wanted to be married, but how did you explain that the man you loved did not want to have children? That you had hoped over the years that he would change his mind, and that he had not? That eventually the distance between you had grown and you knew that the only way out for both of you was to break off the relationship.

Shanna still thought of Tom at times, although it had been three years since she had seen him last. They had parted friends, yet the breakup had been terribly painful. Still, now, years later, Shanna knew she had made the right decision. All she had to do was think of Sammy and know.

She did not tell the village women any of this. They would never believe her. A man who wanted no children? They would not believe such a person could exist.

"I haven't found the right man," she'd said, which was the truth. And yes, of course, she wanted a husband. Of course she wanted children. And of course at twenty-seven she was very, very old... She smiled now at the memory.

"I expect you used to live in the house?" Rand asked, gesturing at the village behind him.

She nodded. "Yes. No water, no electricity. Huge fireplaces. I loved it."

"Are you staying with Bengt?"

"Bengt? No. Is he the one who lives in the house now?"

"Yes. He's a Swedish volunteer."

"I haven't met him yet. I'm staying at the Rhino Lodge, in Nyahururu." It was a small hotel in a nearby town, not fancy, but clean and comfortable, and it served her purposes fine.

"Not exactly the Hilton."

His superior attitude irked her, the presumption that coping in anything less than a five-star hotel was not among her talents.

She gritted her teeth. "No, it isn't, but it's perfectly adequate. And what business is it of yours where I stay, may I ask?"

He shrugged. "Just making conversation," he said casually.

Conversation my foot, she thought. "Why are you here?"

she demanded, feeling her control slip a notch. She raked her hair away from her face. "Haven't you got something better to do? Herd some cattle, hunt some wounded buffalo?"

"Yes, indeed." He shoved his hands into his pockets and considered her coolly. "I've considered your request. You can come to the ranch and talk to the workers."

She stared at him, too surprised to think of something intelligent to say.

"We have an interesting tribal mix," he went on, "in case you're looking for variety—Pokot, Luo, Meru, Turkana."

"You didn't think it would be useful." Suspicion colored her voice.

He shrugged again. "I changed my mind."

He'd changed his mind, just like that. She wasn't stupid, but looking at his face, she knew that Mr. Rand Caldwell wasn't going to elaborate and that asking would be futile.

He glanced at his watch. "Nick rang this morning and asked me to send you a message. He said something came up and he won't be able to make that trip to Mombasa with you this weekend. He said you were planning to drive back to Nairobi on Friday."

She pushed her hair away from her face. "That's what the plan was. It doesn't matter. Maybe we can go next week."

His face tightened. "You can come to the ranch. You might find the accommodations more comfortable."

She studied his hard, unsmiling face. "Are you inviting me to *stay* with you?"

"Yes," he said brusquely.

Something was wrong. Something was going on and she had absolutely no idea what it was. The man did not like her, yet he was asking her to be his guest. He thought what she was doing was ludicrous, yet now he was helping her.

"Why are you doing this?" she asked. It sure wasn't because he was interested in her work.

His face was expressionless, but something flickered briefly in his eyes. "Nick is concerned about you," he said flatly.

She knew he was. Had he asked Rand to take her in? She did not cherish that thought, as if she were some poor lonely waif who needed looking after.

Still, she had the uncanny feeling that that was not the only reason behind Rand's invitation. She stared at him and bit her lip, wondering. No matter what his motivation was, the invitation was interesting.

Here was an opportunity to enter the den of the lion so to speak, and find out more about Rand Caldwell.

Find out more about him? Now why was she thinking that? Why would she even *want* to find out more about him?

Because the man intrigued her. She wanted to know what lay behind that cold, hostile front. An image flashed through her mind. Rand's smiling face as he looked at the little Indian girl dressed up in her party sari.

There was more to him than met the eye.

She straightened and tossed her hair back over her shoulder. "I'd love to stay at your ranch if it will make Nick feel better, and I'm happy to have the opportunity to talk to the women." She smiled politely. "I appreciate your offer."

Again the slight narrowing of his eyes, the flicker of wariness, as if he didn't trust her. What had she done to illicit this negativity from him?

"When would be a good time for me to come?" she asked.

"Anytime." He gave her directions in short, clipped sentences. "I won't be back at the house until tea time, but they'll know to expect you."

"Thank you."

He stared at her for a moment longer, his eyes unreadable,

then he turned without a word and marched across the uneven ground toward his Land Rover. She watched him go, feeling an odd mixture of excitement and trepidation.

The road passed through small villages, patches of green forest and cultivated *shambas*. Women worked in the maize fields and herds of goats and cattle roamed the land. Shanna drove with the car windows open, wanting to feel the air on her skin, smell the sun-warmed land. She'd be covered in red dust by the time she arrived at the ranch, but she didn't care.

Why had Rand invited her? A man who was said to live almost like a recluse. Just because of Nick? Maybe going to this isolated ranch was not such a bright idea. After all, he had made it quite clear that he was not positively inclined toward her. It was not difficult to call up the image of his arctic eyes, his hard face. Even in the heat of the afternoon it made her shiver.

She kept on driving. The wind had freed a strand of hair. It was whipping annoyingly around her face and she tucked it behind her ear. Well, what was life without taking risks?

Finally, she saw the gate, and the huge sign reading Caldwell Ranching Co. The *askari* guarding the gate looked impressive—a tall, muscular man, wearing a uniform and carrying a gun.

"*Jambo,*" she greeted him and he gave her a friendly grin, returning the greeting. The *bwana* was expecting her, he informed her.

It was many miles yet to the house and she looked around carefully, aware now that she was on Caldwell land, a piece of private Africa with rolling hills and virgin forests, gorges and plains.

With increasing excitement she took in everything—the colors of the land, the herd of swift-footed Thompson gazelles, a giraffe in the distance, feeding off a tree. At night, lions hunted here and hyenas skulked around looking for leftovers.

As she reached the gorge, a deep rocky crevice, she saw the house, perched on the edge and for a moment she held her breath. It was built of rough stone and wood and other natural materials. It had a thatch roof and seemed to be part of its rugged surroundings—unpretentious yet magnificent. It was the most wonderful living place she had ever seen and she slowly expelled her breath. A lush, flourishing flower garden sprawled in front of the house, greeting her with a blaze of color.

Paradise. The thought came automatically, and it made her smile. Certainly she should be safe in Paradise.

She stopped the car and dogs came leaping out of nowhere, barking, wagging tails. There were three of them, and she considered them carefully for a moment. They were excited but friendly, she decided, and opened the car door. A tall, dignified African dressed in white emerged from the house, silenced the dogs and greeted her with a smile. His name was Kamau and he had been expecting her.

She was shown to an airy room with a view of the mountains. It was simply furnished and had a brightly colored bedspread and a soft, white sheepskin rug on the polished wooden floor. A small desk stood against one wall, obviously put there for her use. A bowl of fresh flowers adorned the dressing table; not a welcoming gesture initiated by Rand, she was sure.

Her luggage was brought in from the car, and after Kamau had left, she took off her hiking boots and socks and sat on the bed, contemplating her next course of action.

A sound made her turn around and Rand was standing in the door, which she had left open. Her heart made a silly little leap. He looked dusty and tired and she could already see the dark shadow of his beard.

"You have arrived," he stated.

"Yes. This is the most beautiful place I've ever seen." She glanced at the spectacular view and she couldn't help smiling and feeling warmth and joy spread through her at the sight of all that beauty. "Thank you for inviting me."

He nodded, and his gaze left her face and traveled to the pile of suitcases and bags in the middle of the room.

"That's rather a lot of luggage for two weeks," he commented mildly.

She laughed. "I wanted to be sure to be covered for all eventualities." That was one explanation. The other one was that she wasn't staying for two weeks.

He arched one dark brow. "How many eventualities were you expecting?"

She grinned. "I'm very adventurous. Lots, I hope."

The hard line of his jaw was indication that he didn't think much of her reply. She felt herself begin to tense.

"Tea on the veranda in half an hour," he announced. "Through the arched door at the end of the passage," he added, and turned away.

Half an hour. Enough time for a quick shower and some clean clothes.

She had her own bathroom, spacious and charming with a rustic stone floor and gleaming white fixtures. More fresh flowers on a small rattan table, along with a basket of small soaps and other toiletries. Somebody here knew how to make a guest feel comfortable. She showered, washed her hair and dried it with her blow-dryer.

What to wear? Shorts? Long slacks? A dress? She picked out a long slim cotton skirt and a white, sleeveless top that exposed nothing below her collar bones. Very demure, she thought and she looked at herself in the mirror and grinned. A little fresh makeup and she was ready.

Rand was already on the veranda when she arrived, one of the dogs asleep next to his chair. A man in shorts and work shoes sat across from him and was introduced to her as Patrick Collins, the ranch manager. He was about thirty, she guessed, with sandy hair and brown eyes in a tanned face. "Shanna Moore," Rand introduced her. "She's doing research for a university journal in the States."

Patrick was interested and asked questions. "Come meet Rosemary," he said, "she'll help you find the right people to talk to." Rosemary, he said, was his wife. They lived in a bungalow next to the ranch office just outside the workers' village, which was four miles away. Rosemary knew everybody and would love to have her visit.

A teapot, cups and saucers, sugar and milk were set out on a low table. There was a plate of small sandwiches—cucumber and tomato. Very English. And peanut butter cookies, very American.

"These are good," Shanna said, chewing the nutty cookies. "Taste like the ones my mother used to make. Fannie Farmer's cookbook."

Rand's face tightened almost imperceptibly—she had not imagined it. She stared at him, wondering what it was she had said. He took a sandwich and ate it, not looking at her, and began a conversation with Patrick about the cattle dipping the next day and other ranch business matters. His left arm dangled over the armrest of his chair, his hand absently stroking the comatose dog by his side.

She couldn't help looking at his hand, the gentle stroking of his strong fingers.

She listened to the men talk, drinking the strong tea and eating the sandwiches and cookies. It didn't escape her that Rand did not take any of the cookies. Well, maybe he didn't have a sweet tooth.

After the men left to take care of some more business, Shanna decided to get her notes for her article and work on the veranda for a while. Large open doors led into the sitting room and she looked around with fascination at the cheerfully decorated room—bright-colored paintings on the wall,

Arab carpets on the polished floors. No ceiling, but the wooden beams and thatch of the conical roof were visible high overhead, the design a work of art in itself. A huge stone fireplace dominated one wall. The large cane rattan furniture with its thick cushions looked wonderfully comfortable, and a wall of shelves held books and African carvings. Blooming branches of pink and purple bougainvillea were arranged in a large glass jug which perched on a big round wooden coffee table.

This was not a house with cool elegance or showy opulence, but a living place with natural charm and a casual richness of comfort and color. She resisted the urge to linger and examine the artwork and books, feeling a bit indiscreet about it.

Having collected her work from her room, she returned to the veranda, finding Kamau, clearing away the tea things.

"The cookies were delicious," she said in Swahili. "Did you make them?"

He nodded politely. "Yes, *memsab*. I always bake them for visitors." He took the tray and left.

Shanna stared after him. Had there been a touch of sadness in his dark eyes, or had she just imagined it?

"I read that there's a lot of wildlife on the ranch," she said. "Doesn't it interfere with the herds?" She'd seen the humpbacked Borana cattle this afternoon on her way to the house.

She and Rand were having dinner in the dining room and Shanna was trying to keep a conversation going, which was proving quite a challenge.

"Not generally, but sometimes." On occasion a lion would become a problem, killing lambs or calves, and would have to be shot, he told her. He spoke in short, clipped sentences.

"What about poaching? We hear a lot about that these days."

"Not on my ranch. We have a security system with guards who patrol the property boundaries. We haven't had a problem for years."

It was an awkward, stilted conversation. Not a real conversation at all. She was asking questions and he gave answers in an automatic fashion, as if they had rehearsed the lines from a script.

She looked down at her plate of beef in a wild mushroom wine sauce. "This is delicious. Did Kamau cook this?"

"Yes."

"Who taught him how to cook?"

He drained the last of his wine. "My mother," he said curtly. He reached for the wine bottle. "More wine?"

She nodded. "Please."

Nick had told her that Rand had lost his mother when he was a boy. The cook must have started work in the ranch kitchen as a young man. Rand's father had died five years ago, she knew.

From his responses, it was obvious that Rand had no desire to discuss anything remotely personal. She had, however, found out he had grown up an only child and had learned hunting and fishing from his father, had studied in both the U.K. and the States, and had returned to take over the running of the ranch.

"Was it lonely, growing up here?" she asked.

He raised his brows as if the question had never occurred to him. "No."

"Where did you go to school as a child?"

"In Gilgil and Nakuru, boarding schools."

He was not generous with information and seemed intent on keeping a careful distance, which did not make for a relaxing atmosphere. Standoffish, Lynn had called him. Well, he was. She found his reserve unnerving and it took an effort to be her cheerful, friendly self. He was excruciatingly polite and it was obvious that she was far from a treasured guest. She was relieved when the meal was over. Rand pushed his chair back and came to his feet.

"Now, if you'll excuse me, I have some work to do in my study."

"Of course." She stood up as well and he held open the door for her.

"Wait," he said as she moved past him. She stopped, surprised, saw him looking at her left shoulder.

"Your…earring…" he said, and she automatically felt her left ear and found the ring gone. Somehow it must have worked itself loose.

"It's caught in your hair," he said, reaching for it, as she reached for it .

They both froze, their hands gripped together in her hair. Their eyes met and all she could feel was his big hand, his fingers tangled with hers, the warmth of them. The sudden crazy pounding of her heart.

For a moment that seemed like an eternity they simply stood there looking at each other, not breathing. Then they both let go at the same time and the earring slipped lose from her hair and fell to the wooden floor where it bounced harmlessly under a chair. He rescued it from its hiding place and handed it to her, dropping it into her palm without touching her.

"Thank you," she said.

"Don't mention it."

And then she moved past him into the hall and went into her bedroom while he continued to his study.

She sat down on the side of the bed and let out her breath slowly, realizing her body was all tensed up. She unclenched her hands, rubbed her forehead.

This was too nerve-racking for words. Maybe it had been a mistake to come here. Maybe she should have stayed in the hotel in Nyahururu.

No, said a little voice, you were curious about Rand Caldwell.

Impatient with her own thoughts, she came to her feet and picked up the big, padded envelope she'd put on the desk when she'd unpacked her luggage. She opened it and slid out several notebooks and a sheaf of manuscript papers.

Her father's personal journals. Four years of observations, thoughts, notes, and anecdotes, written while living in Kanguli. Like the man he had been, his handwriting was simple and clear and easy to read.

Using the journals, her father had started writing a book for publication. It had only been half-finished when he and her mother had died tragically when a drunken driver had careened into their car at high speed.

It had taken her a long time to gather the courage to read the journals, and once she had, a floodgate of emotion had been opened inside her. He had written about people and animals, about loving and living African-style. The stories were touching or humorous. She had wept and laughed. She had known then, that the book could not go unfinished. Other people would be entertained and inspired by her father's work. It deserved to be shared.

Like the scientist he was, her father had made a detailed outline and plan for the book. She had studied the finished section, discovering that the material was in essence taken straight from the journals, organized and rearranged in a new format.

She had sat at her desk, her hands trembling, her heart pounding. I can do it, she'd thought, and the words had echoed in her head for days like a secret mantra. *I can do it. I can do it. I can do it.*

Her love of writing, of expressing her thoughts and feelings on paper, she had inherited from him. She was her father's daughter and she'd felt the swelling of joy and pride inside her.

I can do it.

She could do it. She was, in fact, uniquely qualified to do it.

And so the planning had begun. She had found a publisher who was interested in the project—in actual fact, she'd found two. She'd made a choice, signed a contract and received an advance large enough to make her stay here possible, backed up with the money from her parents' life insurance policy.

Shanna looked down on the papers and smiled. And here she was, back in Kenya, where her father had begun the journals, and where she would finish the book. In the next few days she'd have to tell Nick that she had decided to stay and was not flying back with him to the States at the end of next week.

She did not want to go back to her apartment where so much reminded her of Sammy. It would be easier to deal with her feelings here, in another environment, doing something interesting. And certainly finishing the book here would be so much easier.

She settled at the desk and switched on her laptop computer. She studied the outline for chapter eight and found the journal entries assigned to it, absorbing the sounds coming from the bush outside through the open window.

Three hours later she came to her feet, stiff and tired, but feeling a great sense of accomplishment. Too keyed up to go to sleep, she quietly slipped out of her room, along the passage to the veranda.

The air was cool and the only light anywhere came from the stars and a half moon. The world was dark and full of sounds—mysterious, frightening. Below in the gorge animals were sleeping, or hunting. It was wild, secret and dangerous out there and she shivered a little.

From the house behind her came footsteps and Rand appeared next to her with a drink in his hand. Her heart made an awkward little leap as she looked at him in the pale moonlight and a thought floated through her mind. Rand was like the gorge below—wild and secret.

And dangerous.

She could sense it, yet not understand it. If he were a threat to her, then why?

It wasn't physical, she knew that. It was a more subtle danger, more insidious, more devastating. He could hurt her.

She shivered again. What made her think like this?

"You're up late," he said evenly.

"I was working. Now I'm too excited to sleep."

"Excited? Why?"

"I still can't believe I'm really back here after all these years. In a way I was afraid."

"Afraid of what?"

"To spoil my memories. I was afraid I would be disappointed."

"And you're not."

"No, oh, no! Not in the least."

A coughing sound came from somewhere in the darkness.

"Leopard," said Rand, "down in the gorge."

Leopard.

She hugged herself.

"Cold?" he inquired politely.

She shook her head. "No, just…I don't know. Overwhelmed, I think. At home I'd hear cats meow or dogs bark. Now, here I am, listening to a leopard."

They were silent for a while, standing there together listening to the mysterious darkness.

She glanced at his shadowed face. "Did you ever think of settling in the States or England when you were there?" she asked.

"No," he said shortly. "This is my home. I can't imagine living anywhere else."

She could well understand it. The place had a hypnotic

atmosphere, a magnetic pull. "I imagine it's too romantic a view, but it seems a wonderful kind of life here."

He gave a short laugh that held no humor. "Romantic indeed. And naive. Not many people can take this kind of wonderful life for very long." His voice held a note of disdain. "Most people need the excitement and stimulation of cities and people around them," he said flatly. "You live in Boston, you must know."

"Yes, but city life can get very stressful. I like to get away. I often do. I enjoy being with people, but I also like to be by myself."

"Where do you go to be by yourself?"

"The beach, the woods, the park. I like to walk. It gives me a chance to hear myself think. I rather like my own company at times."

There was a silence.

She glanced over at him. "Does that sound conceited? That's not how I mean it."

He raised his brows fractionally. "How do you mean it then?"

She frowned. "I think…" What she wanted to say was that she was comfortable with herself, with the person she was. She was not afraid of her own feelings or her own thoughts. She had no idea how she was going to say that without sounding over the top.

"You think what?" he urged.

She took a deep breath. Well, she had to finish what she had started. "I'm comfortable with myself," she said. "I'm not afraid of my own thoughts and feelings." She didn't care what he thought.

"And what does that mean?"

She searched for words. It was a strange conversation to be having with him. "I'm quite aware I'm a flawed human being, but I try to live…honestly, to be aware of other people's feelings and needs, and not to be too judgmental."

That sounded pretty good, but she had to admit that not being judgmental wasn't easy where it concerned Mr. Caldwell.

"Judgmental?"

"It's easy to criticize other people, but you can't tell what's in someone's heart, and you don't always know the reality of someone else's life."

"How very noble," he said, and his voice was coldly mocking. "Is this little speech for my benefit? A less-than-subtle hint perchance?"

His voice chilled her to the bone. "What is that supposed to mean?"

"Don't play the innocent, will you?" He turned and strode back into the house.

Her astonishment overwhelmed even her anger. She had no idea what he had been hinting at. She stood motionless at the veranda railing, staring out into the darkness. Then anger took the upper hand. This was outrageous! This was going too far!

She stormed in after him. "Rand!" she called, and he stopped and turned, hands on his hips. Brows arched sardonically.

"Yes?"

She moved in front of him, heart racing, legs trembling. "I'd like to know what's going on here!" She crossed her arms in front of her chest. "You don't like me. First I assumed it was something general—your not liking women, or just simply having a rotten disposition, but now I know it's more than that. I'm not given to paranoia, but I'm beginning to think that this is a rather personal thing and I'd like to know what you've got against me. You don't even know me!"

"Oh, I know you," he said frigidly. "I know your type."

"My *type?*" It was getting more preposterous by the minute.

"Beautiful, selfish, and deceitful."

She felt her mouth begin to drop open and she clamped her jaws shut just in time. The man was a lunatic! She took a steadying breath.

"If you feel this way, why in the world did you invite me to stay at your house?"

His mouth curved with faint contempt. "To keep you from going back to Nairobi. Nick told me that Melanie arrived unexpectedly, to surprise him."

Melanie was in Nairobi? How was that possible? Nick had tried to persuade her to come along for a while, a week, even just a few days, but she'd not wanted to be away from the kids, not so far. And now she was here anyway? It had to be a mistake.

"Melanie?" she asked, incredulous.

"Yes, Melanie," he bit out. "Nick's wife. You do know he's married?"

"Of course I know he's married! What—"

"Well then, perhaps you'll agree it would be more discreet to stay out of their way?" His icy gaze bored into hers. "Surely you're not totally without scruples?"

CHAPTER THREE

RAND opened the door and marched out as if he could not tolerate being in her presence a moment longer.

Stunned, Shanna sagged into a chair and stared at the door. Suddenly it was all very clear—all the pieces fit. Rand thought she was having an affair with Nick. She was the woman Nick was fooling around with on the side and this trip to Kenya was a perfect opportunity to be together. His own wife was too busy with the children, wasn't she? Shanna could hear Rand's thoughts as if he were talking out loud.

It was so absurd that when the initial shock wore off, she could only laugh. It was too crazy for words.

He was seeing her as a *femme fatale* who'd trapped his poor friend in a web of sin. He did not approve of such immoral behavior. He had standards.

Well, having standards was good. She liked men who had standards. However, judging and condemning others was not such a good idea always. And certainly not when you weren't in possession of all the facts.

For a while she sat in the chair without moving, going over it all again, and the humor faded. No one had ever thought so badly of her, not to her knowledge, and it wasn't a good feeling. What had she done to make him judge her this way?

And then another thought occurred to her.

Why did Rand care? What was it to him who she was? He and Nick hadn't seen each other in years. It was none of his business what Nick did with his private life.

She sighed wearily, feeling suddenly exhausted. Well,

there had been enough upheavals for one day. Perhaps this mystery would be solved later. In the meantime, she was tired and she wanted to go to bed. Tomorrow she'd set the high-and-mighty Mr. Rand Caldwell straight, explain to him that he was quite mistaken in his diagnosis of the situation and that perhaps he should not jump to conclusions quite so quickly in the future.

She awoke to a glorious morning. The open window revealed a square of vivid blue sky decorated with a blooming branch of amethyst bougainvillea which swayed gently in the breeze—like a living painting. She lay still, absorbing the sounds coming from outside—chickens clucking, birds twittering in the bushes. What joy to wake up to such serenity every morning. She let out a languorous sigh.

A soft, tentative knock came on the door. Whoever it was, it wasn't Rand. Tentative was not one of his behavioral characteristics.

"Come in," she invited.

A young girl in a pink cotton dress came in with a tea tray. She smiled, her big eyes looking at Shanna with curiosity.

"Good morning, *memsab*," she said in Swahili. "I have brought you your *chai*." She placed the tray on the bedside table, picked up the small pot and poured the tea in the low, wide cup.

"*Asante sana.*" Shanna smiled back at the girl. She was sixteen or so, and very pretty. "What is your name?"

"Catherine. Please let me know if you need anything."

"Thank you, I will."

The girl withdrew and closed the door behind her.

Shanna looked at the tea. It was very dark. She was used to drinking coffee in the morning, but this seemed to add a touch of authenticity. Tea for breakfast. Very English. She added milk and sugar and contentedly sipped the strong, sweet brew.

After she'd dressed, she found Rand in the kitchen talking to Kamau. Bush hat on his head, keys dangling from his hand, he was ready to leave. For some perverse reason she felt a twinge of disappointment.

Disappointment? What was wrong with her? Did she *want* to sit across from him while she ate her breakfast?

"Good morning," she said, trying to sound light.

His cool gaze barely met hers. "Good morning," he returned in a businesslike tone—a tone so impersonal it set her teeth on edge.

"We have to talk," she said, bracing herself. Might as well get it out of the way.

"It will have to wait," he said and strode out the door without giving her another look. A moment later she heard the car engine start and Mr. Rand Caldwell had departed for the day, she assumed. Well, good riddance.

She ate a solitary breakfast, prepared by the dignified Kamau, sitting on the dining room terrace. The air was crisp and effervescent like champagne. Feeling restless, she decided to go for a walk before settling down to work. Strolling through the garden, she reveled in the joyous color and fragrance of the flowers, the many blooming bushes and trees—frangipani, jasmine, bougainvillea. Who had designed and planned this gorgeous place?

She left the fenced-in garden, but stayed reasonably close to the house, not leaving the established paths, trying to get closer to the gorge. Below pools of water shimmered in the sunlight. Birdsong filled the air, and butterflies fluttered around the blooms. She sat down on a large bolder and surveyed her surroundings with her binoculars.

Not much later she heard a soft rumbling sound, then noticed a dust cloud approaching on the main drive. It was Rand's Land Rover, returning to the house.

He made a sudden right-hand turn, left the road and followed the rough track coming toward her. He must have spotted her, which wasn't difficult since her raspberry-pink sweatshirt was hard to miss. Why couldn't the man leave her alone?

He stopped and leaned his head out of the open window. Not surprisingly, his face did not express joy and frivolity. The hard line of his jaw and the angry look in his eyes promised nothing good.

"What do you think you're doing here all by yourself? Haven't you any sense? This is not the zoo, for God's sake!"

She stiffened involuntarily and felt her hackles rise. Damn, the man had a way of getting to her! She forced herself to stay calm. "I'm quite all right, thank you," she said politely.

He scowled at her. "Get in! I'm going back to the house."

His authoritarian manner infuriated her. "I'll walk back."

His eyes shot blue fire. "I said get in, and I mean it! I won't have you tramping through the bush on your own! You don't know what you're doing."

"You're not responsible for me," she managed to say in a civilized voice. "And I don't like being ordered around."

He cocked a brow, unimpressed. "A couple of days ago a leopard was spotted right over there by the house. You don't want to meet him behind a bush. Now are you getting in or do I throw you in?"

She got in.

He reversed the Land Rover, then turned it around. "If you want to walk, all you need to do is tell Kariuki and he'll go with you," he said. Kariuki was one of the *askaris* guarding the ranch house and its surroundings.

"I used to go walking by myself all the time," she said tightly.

"Not here you won't. Forgive me if I don't have much confidence in your wilderness skills. I don't need an accident on my hands. I've got enough to do."

Of course. "You're quite the lord and master, aren't you?" she said coolly. "Is this the way you treat everybody?"

He ignored her, apparently not finding it worthy of his efforts to respond. She gritted her teeth. His arrogance was insufferable. He assumed too much. He assumed she was stupid, that she was a moral lightweight, that...

Her hands clenched in her lap at the sudden awareness that she did not want him to think so little of her. Helpless anger made her feel like bursting into tears, and the thought that she might actually do so terrified her. She fought the impulse with all her might. The strength of her emotions surprised her. What was wrong with her to react so intensely to this man and his behavior toward her?

Silence reigned. She gazed out over the countryside, contemplating how she could best tell him he was very wrong about her and Nick. The right words, the right time. Taking in a deep, calming breath, she glanced at his profile. Square chin, strong, well-defined lines. A profile that emanated confidence and arrogance.

She wouldn't mind taking him down a notch, but this was not the time. She was upset and the last thing she wanted was to lose her composure. Maybe tonight. She was not a vindictive person, but he had pushed her just a little too far. Mr. Rand Caldwell's behavior was offensive. Nobody had ever accused her of deceitful behavior or questioned her integrity. No one had ever suggested she was having an affair with a married man. No one had ever had any reason to find her guilty of either. And no matter how rational she was trying to be, it unsettled her. She just couldn't help it.

She calmed herself by thinking up interesting scenarios in which she would tell him of his mistake and he would need to apologize for his arrogance and ignorance. One in particular she liked best: Rand on his knees, begging for forgiveness. The image was fascinating, although not in the realm of the possible. Humor winning out over her anger, she grinned at herself. It made her feel much better.

He gave her a quick, sideways glance. "What's so funny?" he asked.

"You," she said, not able to resist. She smiled sunnily.

Something like surprise flickered in his eyes, then he frowned and focused on the road again. There was nothing remotely funny about him and he probably thought she was a complete nutcase, among all the other things he was thinking. His impressions of her must be taking on a nightmarish quality.

They drove up the long drive and he stopped in front of the house. "I'm going back to the office in five minutes," he said. "You can come with me and visit Rosemary and talk to some of the women in the village if you like."

She felt a surge of enthusiasm. "Thank you, yes, I would like that," she said nicely.

The dogs had come bounding out to greet them and Rand patted them each, then stalked off in the direction of his study, with all three of them following him in. In her room, Shanna gathered writing material and was ready to go in minutes flat. She climbed back in the Land Rover and waited for Rand. One thing he wouldn't be able to accuse her of was that she'd left him waiting.

One of the workmen came from behind the house and climbed in the back of the car, giving her a cheerful good morning. He was riding back to the office to fix some problem with a leaking water pipe, he said. Rand emerged from the house carrying some papers, which he handed the man to hold.

They said little during the drive to the ranch office, which was fine by her. She was content to look at the scenery.

At the edge of the workers village Rand dropped her off at the manager's house, a white, thatch-roofed bungalow surrounded by an English-looking flower garden. Patrick's wife, Rosemary, was delighted to see her, and ushered her into a bright, airy living room with interesting paintings and a wall full of books. Rosemary was tiny, with short, sleek black hair and hazel eyes.

Shanna liked her on sight. They talked and talked over coffee and banana cake.

Then they talked some more, had more coffee and more banana cake. They laughed. They looked at each other in happy recognition. Surely they had known each other in a previous life. Or maybe more than one.

Rosemary had managed to carve out a life for herself in this isolated place without perishing from loneliness. She worked in the ranch office three days per week, gave lessons in health and nutrition to the village women, and served as a first-aid health worker to the village population. When aspirin and bandages weren't enough, she would take the patient to the nearest clinic in her car.

They didn't discuss Rand. Rosemary didn't mention him. Shanna didn't mention him.

After a light lunch, they walked into the village and Rosemary introduced her to several of the women. Sitting in the shade of a big tree, she spent a couple of hours chatting and having a wonderful time. Later Rosemary drove her back to Rand's house and she was sorting through her notes when Kamau told her that the *bwana* was on the phone for her.

"I want you to listen carefully," Rand said, and his voice sounded full of dire threat.

She raised her eyes heavenward. "Yes, *bwana*," she said obediently.

"There's a problem," he stated. "Melanie and Nick are

driving up here for a visit. It must have been Melanie's idea and Nick couldn't get her to change her mind.''

Shanna felt a rush of mirth; in spite of everything. She could tell him now not to worry about a thing, that she was not having an affair with Nick. A nasty little devil inside her took over. Shame on her. She, a nicely brought-up girl from Boston.

''There's no problem,'' she said, which was the truth.

''There'd better not be,'' he said darkly.

''I'll be a good girl,'' she promised. ''Don't you worry about a thing.''

There was a slight pause. ''You're good at this, are you?'' he said, his tone dripping distaste.

''Good at what?''

''Handling this sort of situation.''

''Oh, yes,'' she said lightly.

Another pause. ''Well, I warn you,'' he said ominously, ''don't make a wrong move.''

''Oh, I won't.'' Her hand clamped hard around the receiver. It was almost too much to keep this up. ''Tell me, why do you care, anyway? What's this to you?''

''I have no inclination to discuss this despicable situation further with you. I simply suggest you cause no problems.''

She took a fortifying breath. ''I'll cause no problems,'' she said truthfully.

''Good.'' The line went dead.

She put the phone down and found her knees trembling. She groaned and closed her eyes. Rand Caldwell was doing terrible things to her normally steady nerves and she didn't like it.

She went back to her notes, but her concentration was gone. Kamau served tea on the veranda and she sat there, wondering if Rand was really such a monster, or if something more human lurked beneath his hard exterior.

She grimaced and glanced down at her notebook, forcing her attention back on what she had written.

Rand came home an hour later, looking dusty and dirty. She was still sitting on the veranda, and his gaze skimmed her quickly. Her body tensed automatically.

"Working?" he inquired.

"Yes. I had a great time with Rosemary, and with the women in the village." She was going to be polite if it killed her.

He nodded, his gaze settling on something below in the gorge. "Elephant," he said, and she bolted upright to see.

There were several of them, drinking at a water hole. "This is great!" she said breathlessly, looking on in awe at the huge beasts.

They watched in silence until Kamau appeared saying that the guests had arrived. Rand threw her a warning look and anger rushed through her, burning like a swallow of too-hot coffee.

He strode inside to greet Nick and Melanie, returning a few minutes later, alone.

"They're in their room to freshen up. They'll join us later."

She came to her feet. "I'll change for dinner, too." She gathered her papers and went inside, moving through the living room to the passage. Again it struck her how cheerful a place it was and that somehow it didn't make sense: here was a wonderful house with colorful paintings and Arab rugs and a cook who produced lovely dinners; here was a house for love and laughter and its sole occupant was the silent, morose Rand.

The warm, vivacious ambience of the place was a sharp contrast to Rand's personality. It baffled her. Who had decorated the house? Who had put those brilliant paintings on the wall? Those jewel-colored rugs on the floor?

Had it been Marina, the painter, the woman who had lived with him here for a year?

She felt an odd tightness in her chest. Taking a deep breath she hurried down the passage to her room. She had a shower and looked through her clothes for something to wear. For a moment she was tempted to wear her red dress, then conceded that the circumstances were probably not ideal. Shades of scarlet woman. She hung the dress back and found a white one instead. Pure as the driven snow. Well, she was innocent, wasn't she?

When she came back to the veranda, only Rand was there, a drink in his hand. He had changed his clothes, she saw, and his hair was damp from the shower. His gaze swept over her from top to toe and she didn't miss the fleeting glint of admiration in his eyes. No matter what he was thinking of her, he was not immune to her as a woman.

Their eyes met and for an electric moment the feeling was there again, that undeniable attraction, the hidden desire just under the surface. As if suddenly they'd been transported into another reality.

Her heart beat fast, her breath locked in her throat.

She wanted to say something, tell him…

Behind her the wooden floor creaked and Nick emerged onto the veranda. Rand looked away, and the moment had gone. She felt strangely disoriented. What was happening to her?

She looked at Nick. He smiled and gave her a hug, kissing her cheek.

"You look gorgeous," he said.

The world was normal again. She smiled at him. "Thanks."

The next moment she caught Rand's narrowed eyes and the anger was not concealed. She glanced back at Nick. "Where's Melanie?"

"Fighting with her hair," Nick said, rolling his eyes.

"She'll be here in a minute." He looked at Rand. "I hope this doesn't inconvenience you, but she insisted she wanted to see you, and the ranch, and I couldn't refuse. She's ecstatic now that she's here."

"Of course not," said Rand politely. "You two have a standing invitation, you know that. Now, sit down, have a drink."

There was a cart with a collection of bottles, glasses, an ice bucket and other necessities for sundowners. Nick had a Scotch and Shanna asked for a gin and tonic. At home she hardly ever had mixed drinks, drinking only an occasional glass of wine with a meal, but sitting here in Africa, watching the sun sinking and coloring the sky, a gin and tonic seemed the appropriate beverage.

It was cool and deliciously refreshing with its generous squirt of fresh lime juice and she sipped it contentedly, enjoying the breeze stroking her skin. It took several more minutes before Melanie made her appearance. She looked wonderful in a new blue dress, her auburn hair curling enthusiastically around her smiling face. Melanie was not beautiful, but she radiated a warmth that drew people to her.

Shanna came to her feet and they hugged. "I'm so glad you could come," she said. "Are the kids okay?"

"My mom's with them. She practically pushed me out the door." Melanie grinned at Rand. "My mother sends her love. She baked some pumpkin bread for you. I have it in my suitcase."

Surprise flashed across his features. Then he smiled. "Thank you. I can't believe she remembered after all these years." The smile warmed his face and Shanna watched him, realizing that the only other time she'd seen him smile was when he'd looked at the little Indian girl at the party.

"Of course she remembered," said Melanie. "She only made it for you every time you stayed with us."

An hour later they went in to eat their dinner, and again

Shanna noticed how beautiful the table was laid, with flowers and candles and lovely china. It was a relief not to be alone with Rand, but to have Nick and Melanie here to talk to.

The food was delicious and all through the meal, Rand kept looking at her. There was no hiding the easy relationship she had with Melanie and Nick, no hiding the fact that they were close. She wondered what he was thinking, wondered what he might say to her, later.

After coffee, as soon as it was possible to do so without appearing impolite, she excused herself and went to her room, feeling it best to leave Rand alone with his guests. As far as Rand was concerned, her presence was not wanted, and she could do without his icy stare.

Sitting down at her desk, she switched on the computer and called up the file for her article. The sooner she got her material entered, the better. She smiled as she thought of the women she had talked to that afternoon. It had been fun. She loved her work, and working now, at night, was no punishment at all. Besides, she wanted to get the research piece finished as soon as possible so she could send it off and concentrate on her father's book.

It was late and she was about to go to bed when she heard the knock on her door. She came to her feet and opened it.

Rand stood in front of her, eyes cool.

"I want a word with you," he said.

CHAPTER FOUR

"COME in," she said, bracing herself. "I've wanted to talk to you, too."

He leaned back against the door and studied her. "You seem to get on very well with Melanie."

"So I do."

"I imagine that there is the possibility that you're having an affair with Nick right under her very naive and trusting little nose. These things happen, don't they?"

"Yes, they do." She stared right at him, aware she was wearing nothing but a thin nightgown.

"And no doubt it would take a lot of nerve and cold-bloodedness to carry that off successfully."

"Yes." No doubt it would. Not that she had experience having affairs with married men right under the noses of their wives, or otherwise, but it didn't take much imagination to see that it would take considerable skill.

He shoved his hands in his pockets. "Then there are other possibilities. I wonder if you might have another explanation for your relationship with Melanie and Nick."

"I don't owe you any explanation." She felt the hot beginnings of anger and indignation, tried to stop them. "I find your attitude despicable," she said in a low voice, trying to stay calm. "You've judged me without reason." The unfairness of it all suddenly overwhelmed her and her control began to slide. "How dare you! How—"

Her tongue stopped cold as she saw a smile creep around his mouth.

"Aha," he said slowly, "you do have a temper. I won-

dered what it would take to break that cheerfully sophisticated control of yours.''

She clenched her teeth hard. ''You're insufferable,'' she
said. ''Now, do me a favor and leave me alone.''

''Not until this is straightened out. Nick introduced you
as his niece, and I suppose that's exactly what you are.''

''Yes. And what made you think any different?''

''Because it seemed so blatantly not true.''

''You are a cynic, aren't you?''

His expression gave nothing away. ''I made an error in
judgment.''

''Yes, you did. Nick is your friend and you found reason
not to believe him. Has he ever lied to you before?''

He shrugged. ''I imagine you are well aware that he used
to be quite a playboy. Never stuck it out with any one
woman for very long. I'm afraid my confidence in his fi-
delity was a trifle shaky.''

Well, she could not really blame him for his opinion. It
was true enough Nick had played the field when he was
younger, but that was years ago. Nick loved Melanie. There
was no doubt in her mind he'd evolved into a perfectly hon-
orable and faithful husband. Rand, of course, had not been
around to see the two together for years.

''But even so,'' she said tightly, ''his relationship with
me is none of your business.''

''Melanie was my friend before I knew Nick. I did not
want to see her hurt.''

''Were you in love with her?'' The question came automatically.

His mouth quirked. ''No. My feelings for her were more
of the brotherly variety.''

Which might explain some of his behavior, Shanna decided. He'd thought she, Shanna, had been a threat to
Melanie's marital happiness.

His eyes met hers. There was a long silence and her heart began to jump nervously.

"I apologize for misjudging you," he said finally.

He wasn't on his knees and he wasn't begging for forgiveness; this was as close as he was going to come, she was quite sure.

She straightened her shoulders. "All right, apology accepted." She felt very noble, very mature.

"Why didn't you tell me?"

"I tried to, this morning. I didn't have any idea what your problem was until last night and you'd left before I was over the shock and found my tongue."

His brows arched fractionally. "And this evening you were just going to make me figure it out for myself." It was a statement, not a question.

"Yes. When you gave me that charming phone call this afternoon warning me so graciously to behave myself or else, all charity left me, I'm afraid."

His mouth quirked again. "Well, I cannot blame you for that. I'll admit I didn't deserve any charity."

The atmosphere had changed subtly. She was aware, as she was sure he was, too, that the barriers between them had crumbled a bit, if not collapsed completely.

"Nick and Melanie and their kids are the only close family I have," she said, "and I love them."

"Yes, I can tell."

"And I hope you can tell that the two of them love each other, too."

He nodded and straightened away from the door. He looked at her, held her gaze.

Her pulse leaped.

He extended his hand to her. "Again, my apologies."

She took his hand, felt the hardness and the heat of it singing through her blood. "I'm glad we've cleared this up," she said, her voice not quite steady.

"So am I."

He was still holding her hand. The deep blue of his eyes mesmerized her, made her head feel light.

Then he let go and reached for the door handle. "By the way, they'd like to see the animals in the morning. We'll have to get up very early. Is it safe to assume that you'd like to join us?"

It was still dark as she was dressing the next morning. Catherine had awakened her and brought in a cup of tea. Another knock came on the door as she was gathering her hair in a ponytail at the back of her neck. It was Melanie, looking for a belt for her jeans. "I was in such a hurry, I forgot to pack one and these jeans are so loose, it doesn't feel right without one."

Shanna came to the rescue with a belt and Melanie pushed it through the loops of her waistband, yawning. "The only problem with this excursion is that it has to be at this indecent hour of the morning," she said. "And then this sweet girl in pink brings us *tea!*"

Shanna laughed at Melanie's contemptuous tone. "I'm sure she won't mind bringing you coffee if you ask her."

"I did." Melanie examined herself in the mirror as she buckled her belt, then her gaze caught Shanna's. Her eyes narrowed in question. "What is all this iciness between you and Rand?"

"He thought I was having an affair with Nick and he didn't want you to know." Well, there it was, simply said.

Melanie's eyes widened and her mouth dropped open. *"What?"* Then she made a choking sound as laughter won out over surprise. "Oh, no, this is so funny!"

"I'm glad you think so," Shanna said dryly. "It sure wasn't funny for me."

"I'm sorry," Melanie sputtered, not able to control her mirth completely. "Did you set him straight?"

"Oh, yes. Apparently he has some protective brotherly feelings for you. Why is that?"

"Mmm. Well, my family practically adopted him when he was studying in the States. He was my brother's best friend and he spent weekends and holidays with us. He liked our family and he treated me like his cute little sister."

Shanna grimaced. "And when he thought I was having my wicked ways with Nick, all his protective brotherly instincts surged forward."

Melanie laughed. "Such loyalty after all these years. I'm flattered."

"Nice for you, but not so nice for me in this instance. I've never been the victim of such icy contempt."

Melanie groaned. "He apologized, I hope?"

"Yes, he did."

"So what do you think of him?"

"I think my opinion of him is best left unexpressed."

Melanie laughed. "But now you know his soft spot. He's loyal and fiercely protective. Not such a bad character trait in a man."

She could not argue with that. "Why isn't he married?"

Melanie looked thoughtful. "I have no idea. It's not something you ask in a Christmas card. I don't remember him ever talking about his deeper feelings, not the real personal stuff, you know. But then, many men have trouble expressing themselves. And he definitely has that kind of British reserve about him, don't you think?"

"Oh," said Shanna slowly. "Is *that* what that's called?"

Melanie looked thoughtful. "He's a good man, Shanna. Really."

Shanna sighed. "I've been trying to see the humor in this situation, but I can't help feeling...I don't know, diminished. Why would he think that of me? I mean, from the moment he laid eyes on me in Nairobi. What did I do?"

"Maybe it isn't you at all, you know. Maybe it's his own

prejudices or preconceived ideas that made him act that way. Maybe something totally innocent triggered something in his mind. Who can tell?''

A pounding came on the door, and then Nick's voice inquiring if his darling wife had solved her fashion problems and what was keeping the two of them anyway.

Shanna opened the door, smiled nicely at Nick and informed him that they'd been talking about men, as women do all the time, unless they talk about clothes, or children. And yes, they were ready to go look at the wild animals now.

During the next few days, the four of them explored the ranch, Rand taking them by Land Rover as well as on foot over hills, through valleys and gorges and across the grasslands. An armed African tracker accompanied them, a skinny, quiet man with sharp eyes that caught every twitch and twitter in the landscape.

They saw elephants, rhinos, buffalo, and many eland, and several lions napping in the shade of a tree. Thomson's gazelles, impala, warthogs and giraffes were easy to spot. It was all very exciting and Shanna felt alive and happy.

Rand was the perfect host, and now that the hostility between them had eased, she noticed in him a more relaxed nature. He even smiled and laughed at times. He would touch her hand, her arm, to get her attention when he wanted to point something out to her. He kept looking at her, and it was hard to miss the vibrations between them, an unmistakable electricity sparking in the air.

Something magical was happening in those sunny days as they roamed the bush. She listened to his voice, watched his big hands on the Land Rover's steering wheel, the sharp, keen look in his brilliant blue eyes, the tough, muscled strength of his body as he leaped out of the Land Rover. She loved the effortless ease with which he moved over the rough terrain, rifle slung over his shoulder, eyes ever-watchful.

And something wild and wonderful grew inside her—wild and wonderful like the bush and the animals and the endless Kenya sky. Something that made her emotions light, her body restless and feverish. She felt a heightened awareness of the splendor of the land, and the splendor of the man who belonged there, was part of its magic.

It took nothing to set her heart soaring, to make her blood run wild—his intense blue eyes meeting hers for a fleeting moment, an accidental brush of his body against hers.

Some primitive force had taken possession of her, right here in Paradise.

"I don't want to leave," Melanie said to Shanna as she carelessly tossed some clothes in her suitcase. Nick had to get back to work in Nairobi and Shanna was keeping Melanie company while she packed.

Melanie glanced around the room and sighed. "I like it here. I wanted to see this place so much, I can't believe I really know what it's like now." She rolled up a pair of socks and stuffed them in a corner. "Rand told us so much about it when he used to stay at our house and every time I read or heard something about wildlife safaris in Kenya I had to think about this place."

"That's why your mom made sure you could go. And I'm glad you came."

Nick came into the room to pack his suitcase as well.

"I want to tell you something," Shanna said, knowing she could no longer postpone telling them her plan. "I've decided to stay in Kenya."

Nick looked at her with a frown. "I had a hunch that's what you were up to," he said, his voice mildly accusatory.

"Oh, Shanna," said Melanie, "you'll be all by yourself."

"I think what I need is to be away for a while, to be in

a different place and keep my mind busy. And I do think that finishing the book here will work so much better than at home.''

Melanie looked worried, and Shanna understood it well enough. She'd been witness to her crisis—the days of crying and not eating, the sleepless nights wandering through the house. Crying, crying.

But that was over now, the worst of it anyway. Sammy was fine. For her own peace of mind she had to accept that.

Nick sighed. ''We're not going to talk you out of it, are we?''

She smiled. ''No, you're not. But I really don't want you to worry about me. I'll be fine. I'm tough, you know.''

He offered her a crooked smile back. ''Yes, you are.''

''Where will you stay?'' asked Melanie with a worried frown.

''I'll stay at the Rhino Lodge in Nyahururu and look for a place to rent.'' She got up from the side of the bed. ''I guess I'd better start packing, too.''

There was no reason to stay on at the ranch now, and she could not impose on Rand's hospitality any longer. This was his home, not a hotel. She sat on the bed, looking at the opened suitcase, not yet packed.

She didn't want to leave.

It was suddenly an unbearable thought to leave behind this room, this gorgeous place, the views if the hills. Rand.

She closed her eyes. She did not want to leave Rand.

If she did, she would not see him again. He spent his time at the ranch. She wouldn't run into him shopping in the market in Nyahururu, or sipping a drink at the Lodge.

She sat on the bed, unable to stir herself and start her packing. A knock on the open door almost startled her and the subject of her musings stood in the doorway, a glass of brandy in his hand.

"Come in," she said, coming to her feet.

He glanced at the open suitcase on the bed, then back at her.

"Nick told me you've decided not to go back to the States with them. Something about a book you're writing."

"That's right."

He gestured at the suitcase. "Where are you going?"

"I'll get a room at the Lodge in Nyahururu until I find a place to rent. I want to stay near the village."

He nodded, saying nothing.

"I want to thank you for your hospitality," she said, forcing her voice into a light, cheerful tone. "It was wonderful being here, seeing this place."

"You don't need to leave just because Nick and Melanie are. You're welcome to stay until you've found your own place," he said. His tone was even.

Her heart gave a little leap. He was being the gentleman. "Thank you, but I don't want to impose and the Lodge is perfectly fine."

He looked into her eyes. "You won't be imposing. It's no problem."

There was a silence between them, and it throbbed with a breathless waiting. They stood looking at each other. She felt overwhelmed by the strength of her feelings.

She hadn't wanted to leave, and now he was asking her to stay, if just for a little while. He was just being polite.

Maybe.

Maybe he wanted her to stay.

But if she left it would all be over.

She wished she could look inside his head and wonder what he was thinking. What he felt for her. But he just stood there, cool and composed, in charge of his universe.

She had no choice. The only way to find out was to stay here. She had never felt like this before—this sense of destiny. As if this simple decision, giving a yes instead of a no would change the course of her life.

"I'd like to stay," she said and there was a husky tone in her voice that she had not intended. She hoped he hadn't noticed.

He gave a slight nod. "Good," he said, as if a business deal had been successfully concluded. "I'll see you in the morning. Good night, Shanna."

"Good night."

She sat on the bed and felt elation spread through her. She wasn't leaving!

It was a beginning. What she wanted more than anything was to thaw out his cool composure. Cool composure wasn't all there was. Underneath feelings and passions smoldered; she could sense it. There was no mistaking the vibrations between them and she wondered what would happen if she would simply throw her arms around him and kiss him.

It was an exhilarating thought.

It was a dangerous thought.

He could give her a look, a well-chosen word and humiliate her to the depths of her silly soul. He would be capable of that. She would have to be careful and not do something really stupid.

Rand stalked down the passage to his study, berating himself. What the hell was he thinking of? Had he lost his mind?

So she wasn't the loose piece he'd thought she was. So she was gorgeous and sunny and smart. Did that mean he needed her in the house?

The sound of her voice, singing in her room. The way she'd charmed Kamau, showing interest in his cooking, his life. Making him laugh. The colors of her clothes—ruby red, tangerine, jade green, cobalt blue. Her enthusiasm at being here, her interest in the ranch, the animals, the paintings on the walls.

For as long as it would last, he thought cynically.

He felt his insides twisting painfully. On a wave of memory came the sound of piano music, the scent of violets. Twenty years since he'd last seen his mother, so why was he thinking of her now?

Because of Shanna.

Shanna was trouble with her happy smile and green eyes.

And he had invited her into his house.

He slammed the door shut behind him.

Well, it was only for a short time.

CHAPTER FIVE

IT WAS very quiet after Melanie and Nick had gone back to Nairobi. Rand left early every morning to go to work, and Shanna saw little of him in the next few days except sometimes at mealtimes. She worked on the final draft of her article and reread her father's notes.

In the meantime she tried not to think too much of Rand.

She drove into town and scouted around for a place to rent. The only suitable house was a small bungalow that would not be available for another three months. She had coffee at Rosemary's house, spent some more time with the women in the workers' village, drinking *chai* and playing with the children. In the mornings she took long walks in the bush accompanied by Kariuki who was happy to answer her many questions.

She thought too much of Rand.

Every time he walked into the house and his blue eyes met hers, her heart skittered. At night she dreamed of him. She was eternally grateful dreams were private affairs.

''Tell me about that book you're writing,'' he said one evening as they were having their after-dinner coffee.

She told him about her father's notes and journal, and the book he had been writing when he died and left unfinished.

''It's all about people and animals and his work. When I read it, it's like he becomes alive again,'' she said slowly. ''It's as if I can hear his voice, see him stand there with his bush hat on, see him smile.'' She swallowed. ''His writing— it's so vivid, and his insights and thoughts were so... enriching. They're funny and sad and thoughtful.'' She

65

jumped up from her chair. "I have something I'd like you to read."

She rushed into her room, ruffled through the manuscript and found the two pages she had in mind, the ones relating a conversation between her father and a very old, dignified Kikuyu chief.

"Here," she said, handing Rand the pages. "This will give you some idea."

He read them quickly, and to her delight she saw his face ease into a smile, and then he laughed. In the exchange, the clever chief had gotten the better of her father, who didn't mind admitting it and making fun of himself.

"That's very good," he said. "Your father was clearly a keen observer of people and he knew how to put it on paper."

"Yes, and that's why I couldn't let it be, you know. I couldn't let it sit in a drawer and gather dust. It took me a long time to realize what I had to do about it, that I had to finish the book. For him, for myself."

He looked at her thoughtfully. "And you couldn't finish it at home?"

"I tried to do it at home, I did most of the drafting, but it was…I don't know, hard. I really wanted to see the village again, talk to the people to get the feeling right, to be able to capture the light, the scents, the sounds, the colors. It is all so different here, so unique."

"How long will it take you?"

"I don't know. Six months, maybe longer. It's hard to tell at this point."

"It's a long time to be away from home, from family and friends."

She nodded. "But right now I'm probably as free as I'll ever be."

For almost a year she had not been free at all, taking care of Sammy, and if she had the choice…

She didn't want to think about Sammy right now, about what could never be. It hurt too much. She hesitated. "And…well, I needed a change of scenery."

He was looking at her intently, saying nothing and she knew what he was thinking: man trouble, a broken heart. But of course he was too discreet to ask, which made her smile a little.

"I'm not here to recover from a broken love affair," she said lightly.

"And there's no one waiting for you at home?"

"A man? No." She felt herself smile. "I'm an old, old spinster with no hope left, according to my friends in Kanguli. The women my age are all married and have scores of children. They're all feeling very sorry for me."

"You don't strike me as the pathetic type," he said dryly, "nor desperate."

"Not yet, anyway." She made a face and gave a little laugh. *And you don't seem too desperate, either,* she wanted to say, *and you're even older than I am.* Something kept her from saying it out loud.

"Nick doesn't think much of my staying on here to finish the book," she said instead. "He thinks I'm being romantic, unrealistic, et cetera—you get the picture."

"Yes, I get the picture."

She lifted her eyebrows. "You agree with him?"

He shrugged. "You're an adult. You can do as you please. It's not Nick's business whether you stay here or not."

True enough. "Do you think I'm misguided? Romantic?"

"You'll find out. It's a different life here and your experiences were those of a child, and I imagine they've colored your memories." He made a dismissive gesture. "If you don't find what you're looking for, it's easy enough to catch a plane out of here."

There was a sudden coolness to his tone, like an unexpected breeze stirring up leaves, chilling her skin.

"I know what I'm doing," she said, hugging herself without thinking. "I want to stay here, finish my father's book. It's important to me."

And I don't want to go back to my empty apartment in Boston.

"I want to show you something," Rand said early the next morning when she was ready to go out for her daily hike in the bush.

He took her down a narrow, wooded trail nearly overgrown with thick shrubbery. She walked behind him, watching his broad back, the confident stride. She had not been here before and she wondered where he was taking her, all the while keeping her eyes open and listening to the sounds coming from the thick thorny brush along the path. They walked for twenty minutes until they arrived at a clearing and a small water hole.

"Here," he said, pointing at the huge tree nearby, and there amid the leafy branches was a lookout, a wooden platform with a roof.

"Oh!" she said, delighted. "What a great place to watch!"

"I used to come here when I was home from school on weekends sometimes and spend the night," he said.

"Alone? Your father allowed you?"

"I had my gun, and a radio so we could make contact. And sometimes I'd bring a friend from school."

They climbed up to the lookout and sat there, close together in the small space, silently taking in the view.

It was wonderful to see the water hole from this height, although it was already a bit late to expect much animal traffic. She scanned the shrubbery and caught the flicking tail of a tiny antelope, warily approaching the water. Soon it was gone. Then a lone male lion wandered onto the scene, looking sleepy. He drank, then sank lazily down by the side of the water and yawned expansively.

The liquid warbling of birds thrilled in the air. So peaceful it all seemed. So perfectly beautiful. A cloud of butterflies fluttered by.

She wondered why he had taken the effort to show her this place. "Do you mind if I come here on my own sometime?" she asked. "With Kariuki, of course," she added hastily.

"That's why I'm showing it to you," he said. "I thought you might like to just be here once in a while, soak up some ambience for your book."

"Yes, I would, thank you."

Rand was so close, she could feel the warmth of his arm near her own. She wanted to sit here forever, feeling this sense of timelessness, of sweet enchantment.

The air around them was vibrant with tension. She was aware of the vastness of the bush around them, teeming with unseen life, and the fact that the two of them were alone in this beautiful and dangerous Eden.

Slowly he turned to look at her. Their gazes locked and her breath caught in her throat. She could feel the quick dancing of her heart, felt her body tingling as if seduced by the magic of an ancient love spell.

She wanted to touch him, to make sure he was real. She looked into the blue depths of his eyes, wide as the savannah sky, drowning in the vastness. It was like nothing she had ever experienced before, this sense of time standing still, of being conscious of nothing but the moment, the sensation of a magical connection between them.

She wanted him to touch her, slowly.

Not so slowly.

She could barely breathe, the air between charged with sexual energy.

She saw the reflection of it in his eyes, the shadowing of the blue, and her heart turned over.

All he had to do was reach out and take her hand... Move his face only inches closer and kiss her.

He did neither of these things. He just looked into her eyes, holding her gaze. What was he waiting for?

What was *she* waiting for? Couldn't she just as easily reach out to him?

She felt her body began to tremble and she glanced away quickly, at the water hole.

The lion came slowly to his feet, gave an imperious flick with his tail and sauntered off into the undergrowth.

Wispy clouds drifted in the sky. High, high up, a tiny jet hummed through the endless blue. One of the morning flights to Europe—KLM to Amsterdam, British Air to London. To cities full of big buildings and noisy traffic and rushing people.

"We'd better go," said Rand, his calm voice betraying nothing.

After another house-hunting trip two days later, Shanna was on her way back to the ranch. As she approached the house, a small airplane flew over very low, circled the house and disappeared from view behind the thorn trees where the landing strip was.

Curious, Shanna drove on past the house to the strip to see a woman jump from the little plane. She wore jeans and a plain white shirt and a necklace of big amber beads. She looked gorgeous.

"Hello!" she called out with a wave of her hand, coming up to the car with a long-legged stride, red hair shooting sparks in the sunlight.

"Hi," Shanna returned.

"I'm Antonia," the woman said with a smile, extending her hand. "And you must be Shanna."

Apparently news traveled fast here in this vast and empty place. She nodded and took the proffered hand. "Yes. Do you want a ride to the house?"

"Thanks." Antonia opened the door and jumped into the passenger seat. "I'm on my way to Nairobi. I thought I'd stop by to say hello and beg lunch."

Have plane, will drop by for lunch. How easy it seemed. Shanna laughed. "I have no idea who you are," she said.

"I'm Rand's worst nightmare," she said darkly, then laughed. "Just joking."

Shanna had no idea what to think of this, and let it drop.

The dogs welcomed them with happy barks and wagging tails when they drove up to the house, and it was only minutes later that Rand arrived as well.

Antonia greeted him enthusiastically, kissing him on the cheek, European-style—right, left, right—saying she hadn't seen him in ages and why had he not come to the party in Naivasha and he was turning into a recluse and people were *talking* about him. Then again, there was hope, since here she'd caught him red-handed with a *woman* in the house.

"Shut up, Antonia," he said mildly.

"I will not," she said bravely. "And what's more, I'm not leaving here until you've promised that you will come to my party next week Saturday. I will expect a ten-minute speech from you in which you will pour out all your sincere congratulations, admiration, adulation and—"

"For what?"

She sighed and looked wounded. "You don't know? How can you not know? *Everybody* knows."

"Please, don't keep me in suspense," he said dryly. "I'm starving."

From the ensuing conversation Shanna learned that Antonia was a documentary filmmaker and that one of her films had received a prestigious international award. That she had regrettably not been present to receive it because...

Shanna didn't hear all the details, watching instead the animated face, the wild red hair, the dark eyes, the way Antonia used her hands while she talked.

"And when did you hear about this?" Rand asked her.

Antonia glanced at her watch. "Two hours ago."

"And you're sure *everybody* knows about this?"

"All right, all right. Maybe not everybody." She grinned, practically bubbling over. Rand congratulated her, smiling, saying she deserved it. Shanna congratulated her.

They sat down to lunch on the terrace and Shanna learned that Antonia was married to a ranch owner farther up country. They talked about the film, about the party, and Antonia smiled at Shanna and said she was very welcome as well and how long was she staying in Kenya?

Shanna told her about the book, that she was looking for a place to stay in Nyahururu.

And as such things go, Antonia happened to know the perfect place, not too big, with a gorgeous little garden, fully furnished. "They're friends of mine," she said of the owners, "and they're looking for someone to house-sit while they're gone." They were both going to be guest lecturers at the University of California at Berkeley. "You will love the place! It's perfect!"

"When are they leaving?" Shanna asked.

"Next week. I spoke to them just yesterday and they're quite anxious to find someone. I'll call them from Nairobi tonight, tell them to get in touch with you, okay?"

"Thank you," said Shanna, knowing she should feel really, really lucky.

She didn't.

She hadn't really wanted to find the perfect little place.

Two days later she was thinking once again that she should feel really, really lucky because the house was, indeed, perfect. Bright, airy, with comfortable furniture, and a lovely garden. It had a wonderful veranda, perfect for working on her laptop.

"It's very nice," she told Rand that evening. "I can move in next week."

"That worked out very well, then."

"Yes, it did." Only she wished it hadn't. She glanced around the room. "Who decorated this house?" she asked.

He shrugged. "It's always been this way, give or take a few changes now and then."

"Your mother did it, then?"

"I assume she did. Interior decorators probably weren't thick on the ground here when she came to this country."

"It looks very inviting and comfortable and I love those big cushions and these wonderful carpets. She must have been a lovely person with a very, personal style."

He came to his feet and threw another log on the fire, making no response. She stared at the back of his head. Had she said something wrong?

She couldn't sleep that night. She listened to the sounds coming from the darkness, knowing that she'd be gone from the ranch in another week. Knowing she wouldn't see much of Rand after that.

Rand, who had asked politely about the house, then dropped the subject and discussed other matters as if he didn't care that she was leaving.

I'm not in love with him, she told herself. I can't be, not really. Falling in love wasn't something she'd ever done very easily. She'd always had plenty of male friends, but serious relationships took time and effort. And even then they did not always end happily. Love was serious business.

And exciting and exhilarating, of course, she added in her mind.

But she wasn't in love. Just mildly infatuated, slightly smitten, a tad moonstruck.

She groaned into her pillow. Everytime he entered a room,

everytime his eyes met hers, her pulse began to race, her body stirred with irrepressible yearnings.

And she knew he felt it, too, the vibrations between them, the tension in the air. The strength of her emotions frightened and excited her both.

So, who was she fooling?

She stirred, her body restless, thinking about him sleeping in a room nearby, fantasizing…

Thinking about what Lynn had said about the women panting after Rand. Naive idiots, she'd called them.

They all think they're the one who'll have what it takes to break through his reserve and discover the passion underneath.

So she was one more of those naive idiots, was she?

She sat up in bed and rubbed her face. No, she wasn't. This was ridiculous. The sooner she was out of here, the better. And she was going to keep her dignity intact and not throw herself at him like some lovesick puppy and beg him to please let her stay.

Such brave thoughts.

An hour later she was still awake. The room seemed to close in on her and it was driving her crazy. She'd go sit on the veranda and contemplate the universe for a while.

Pulling on a robe against the cool night air, she slipped quietly out of the door and down the passage to the veranda.

"Nice night," came Rand's voice behind her, nearly scaring her silly.

"Where did you come from?" she asked.

"I followed you. I thought I heard something and—"

"I hardly made a noise!" she protested.

He gave a crooked smile. "That's what you think," he said mildly.

Well, of course, she thought then, feeling foolish. The man knew how to track game in the bush; he had the ears of a hunter. He'd hear her breathe from a mile away. He could follow her without her noticing.

She hoped he couldn't read her thoughts as well.

He stood next to her at the veranda railing, wearing only a pair of khaki shorts. In the silvery moonlight his bare chest looked strong and sexy, the kind of chest you'd long to put your cheek against.

Don't go there, she told herself. Don't be a naive idiot.

"I couldn't sleep," she said for something to say.

"Neither could I."

The words hung in the air between them. Her breathing grew shallow, as if she were waiting for something, trying not to make a sound, listening.

"I'd like it if you stayed here," he said then.

It was a simple statement, a simple sentence, but it set her heart racing. And then she felt his hand on hers where it rested on the railing. It was hard and warm and big and her blood pumped wildly through her. She swallowed.

"Why?" she asked.

"Kamau told me to ask you."

She stared at him, feeling her heart crashing. "Kamau?" This wasn't exactly what she'd wanted to hear. "Do you usually do what your servants tell you to?"

"Sometimes." She heard the smile in his voice. "Kamau tells me the house is sad without a woman and since you've been here the house smiles again."

She should feel flattered, at least by Kamau. "And what do you think?"

"I think he's right."

Well, it was something, if not the stuff romance was made of. She was silent and they looked at each other, his hand still covering hers.

"I like your company," he said quietly.

Her heart skipped a beat. Plenty of people liked her company, but coming from Rand, the words took on more significance.

"Coming from a hermit, that's quite a compliment," she said lightly, and he raised his brows fractionally.

"A hermit?"

"Well, maybe not," she said casually, turning her hand under his so she could twine her fingers with his. His hand enveloped hers and her body grew warm. It felt so good to be touched by him, to know he wanted to touch her.

A half moon hung hopefully over the hills and the breeze blew in forgotten scents she longed to know again. The air was vibrant with the chorus of insects and tree frogs—so much life going on in the secret of the night.

"I love this place," she said then. "I'd like to stay."

"Because of the place?" he asked mildly.

Again the little devil stirred in her and a bubble of mirth rose to the surface.

"And because I like Kamau. He's a prince." It was too good to pass up.

"Excellent," he said, not missing a beat. "I like everyone under my roof to get on."

He was good, she had to give him that. She smiled into the darkness.

"Any other reasons?" he asked lightly, and she looked up into his shadowed face and gave him a half smile.

"And I like your company."

"Good." He was still holding her hand. A sudden fresh waft of wind stirred her hair, her face, carrying the scent of jasmine like a promise. She was acutely aware of his nearness and she knew that if he came any closer she'd go up in flames.

He reached up with his free hand and gently took a loose strand of her hair and tucked it behind her ear, his fingers trailing down along her jawline, up from her chin to her mouth.

She stood absolutely still, afraid to breathe as she felt his finger softly tracing the outline of her mouth. She opened her lips, needing air, needing to breathe and then his mouth came down on hers, as she knew it would.

CHAPTER SIX

ALL the days and nights past had been filled with the yearning for his touch and her body responded with a natural recognition as if it had done so many times before.

A soft moan escaped her as she felt the heat of his mouth. All was feeling and sensation—heat and urgency and fire…her body flooded with need…his tongue dancing with hers.

She could not think. Only feel. His arms around her, his body hard and hot against hers…

Breathless wanting, trembling desire, his mouth hungry on hers, his hand sliding over her body, touching her…

He drew back suddenly, and she reeled with the shock of it, feeling bereft, aching.

"Rand…" she whispered. Don't stop, she wanted to say, but the words would not come. Her legs trembled and she held on to the railing, trying not to crumple at his feet like a rag doll.

"I'm sorry," he said roughly. "That was probably not one of my brighter moves."

She swallowed, her mind and thoughts stumbling. "I…I don't know what you mean." What was wrong with him kissing her? As far as she was concerned it was a brilliant move.

It made her feel wonderful. She wanted it to go on. Feel the magic of it, the sense of bliss. She wanted to put her arms around him, kiss him back into the mood of abandon and forgetting, but something inside her, a sudden shyness, kept her from doing it.

He frowned at her. "It wasn't my intention to suggest that there were certain…strings attached to your staying here."

Strings attached. Like sleeping with him in turn for his hospitality.

"Oh," she said, not very brightly.

"Oh, what?"

"I, uh…the thought had not occurred to me." No thoughts of any sort had occurred to her.

"Well, good."

She felt a sudden tickle of amusement and bit her lip to stop from smiling. "Very naive of me, I suppose."

The corner of his mouth quirked upward. "You, a sophisticated city girl."

"You might find it surprising, but not all women are automatically suspicious and distrustful of men and their intentions."

"That is a relief to hear," he said dryly. "And you are one of them, I take it?"

"I suppose I am." She'd had her ups and downs in relationships with men, and the breakup of her relationship with Tom had caused her deep anguish, but no one had ever treated her with disrespect or callousness. Maybe she was lucky. Maybe she just wasn't attracted to the bad type. Or maybe the bad type wasn't attracted to her.

"Well, I'm honored you don't mistrust my long-term intentions." He glanced away into the darkness. "However, it is a beautiful night and neither one of us is substantially dressed, so let me warn you that as for my intentions of the moment, you might want to be a trifle less trusting."

"I'm quite sure you have your animal instincts well under control," she said, not feeling her physical safety was in any danger. If he'd wanted to have his caveman way with her, he'd had plenty of time and opportunity.

"And what makes you think that?"

"Because you're talking rather than acting, as in dragging me off to bed with you, by the hair, or over your shoulder."

She heard him chuckle. "An interesting image. And would you like that?"

"No." Not the dragging part, anyway.

He laughed. "Then I'll have to think of some other approach."

She couldn't think of a reply to that other than, *Please do, right now,* but something kept the words inside her. She said nothing and for a moment there was just the silence and darkness around them and the lightness and humor faded away into the night. She was very aware of him, the nearness of his body, the nervous beating of her own heart.

She wished he would kiss her again, wished she had the courage to put her arms around him and kiss him. She didn't know what kept her from just doing it. There was something in this big quiet man with his penetrating blue eyes that made her feel uncharacteristically timid.

The night air was cold and she gave a little shiver. She felt his hand on her arm.

"You'd better go inside, see if you can get some more sleep." Not the words of a dangerous predator.

"Yes." And then, gathering all her courage, she stood on tiptoe and kissed him quickly on the cheek. "Thank you for inviting me to stay," she said, and rushed inside, back to her room like an embarrassed child.

Somehow, she slept, reliving the kiss in her dreams in vivid detail. When she awoke, the first thought in her head was Rand, and the joyous chirping of the birds outside resonated with her own happy state of mind.

She took no time lingering, jumped out, rushed through her ablutions, dressed and dashed out of the room. She calmed her speed to a more sedate pace as she neared the breakfast room.

It was empty. A used plate and coffee cup lounged forlornly on the table. She stared at them silently, feeling let down, feeling silly.

Kamau appeared in the door. "Good morning, *memsab*."

"Good morning, Kamau. Mr. Caldwell has left already?"

"Yes, *memsab*. Shall I prepare your breakfast now?"

"I'm not very hungry right now. Could I just have some fruit, toast and coffee, please?"

The morning had suddenly lost its shine and she didn't feel like eating Kamau's big English breakfast of bacon and eggs and sausage, not to speak of the sautéed mushrooms and grilled tomatoes that always accompanied it.

She worked on her book all morning, sitting on the veranda, trying valiantly to concentrate and not think about kissing Rand in the middle of the night.

Shortly after noon she heard Rand's Land Rover drive up to the house and her heart made a little leap of joy. She met him on the dining room terrace where lunch was laid out.

"Hi," she said and smiled at him. He looked so good to her—lean and strong and rugged, with the dust of the bush on his boots and his eyes so intense, it made her knees weak.

"Hello," he returned, giving her only the briefest smile before sitting down at the table.

She felt a ripple of disappointment. Well, she thought, that was encouraging. She sat down across from him.

"This looks good," she said, surveying the chicken salad on the table, the platter of sliced tropical fruits.

"Yes," he agreed.

She spooned some of the salad onto her plate and handed him the bowl.

"Thank you."

It was not promising to be a riveting conversation.

"Is something wrong?" she asked.

He shook his head. "No, nothing."

"I'm going into Nyahururu this afternoon," she said as

they began to eat. "Is there anything I can do for you there? Buy something, pick up something?"

He glanced up. "No, thank you."

She'd have to find herself a car to buy, get rid of the rental which was horrendously expensive. And of course she'd have to tell the house owners she would not be renting the house after all. She felt a little guilty about that.

Rand seemed distracted and aloof. They ate in silence and she was aware of the tension between them, unseen but real, like a scent in the air. She thought about how he had kissed her last night, and how he'd seemed...different then. More approachable somehow. Maybe under cover of darkness he found it easier to be more congenial, not to speak of romantic. A nocturnal prowler, so to speak.

Maybe he was sorry he'd kissed her, worried he'd given her the wrong idea.

Which would be what?

That he wanted her?

It certainly had appeared so last night, and she had not exactly rebuffed him either. She'd practically...

Never mind, she told herself, eat your mango.

"This is wonderful," she said, tasting the luscious fruit. She had to say something, anything; she couldn't stand the silence, it was driving her crazy.

"Yes," he said absently and she wanted to throw her water at him.

She wanted to throw herself at him, kiss the silence out of him, hold him hard against her, feel his hands on her.

This was not a good train of thought. She ate some more mango.

In India, she'd read somewhere, mango was highly revered as a love fruit, was supposed to possess aphrodisiac powers. She picked up the platter and held it out to Rand. "Have some more."

"No, thank you," he said, and came to his feet.

In the next few days she saw little of Rand except at dinnertime when he seemed preoccupied and spoke little.

Was he avoiding her? Oh, yes, he was.

Every time she heard his Land Rover drive up, every time she saw him stride into the room, tall, handsome and sexy, her heart leaped. His blue gaze would meet hers. Her heart would leap some more. Then a few words of greeting, some polite enquiries about her day, and that was the end of that.

She couldn't stand it. What was wrong with him?

For that matter, what was wrong with her? Did she have to sit here helplessly pining for his attention like a lovesick teenager?

No she didn't. She had work to do, a book to write. Her research project was finished, the paper sent off to Boston. She was looking forward to spending all her time now on her father's book. Amorous attention from Rand would only be a distraction. Love affairs took so much time, so much energy. She was better off without it.

So she told herself.

Now, if she could actually believe it, she'd have it made.

Rand had had a rotten day, with one problem after another wearing down his patience, topped off with the news that two young cows were found missing when the *wachungai* had rounded up the herd into the *boma* for the night. A search was under way, and he'd been out for two hours himself without success. The animals would find certain death in the African night where predators would find them if people did not.

He was tired and filthy and in need of food. And a stiff drink.

He strode into the house, not in the mood for social pleasantries. He put away his gun, went to wash his hands and stalked down the hall to the veranda, not sure if he wanted to find Shanna there or not.

Shanna with the lush mouth and cheery smile. Shanna with the green eyes. No, he wasn't up to seeing her, talking to her, looking at her bright face. He hoped she was not there, on the veranda.

She was there. Wearing a shirt the color of cayenne pepper.

Crying.

His heart made a sickening lurch. She was sitting in a chair, her hand in her lap holding a picture and copious tears were quietly dripping down her cheeks.

In two steps he stood in front of her. "Shanna?"

She lifted her face, wet with tears, her eyes big with the shock of seeing him. She opened her mouth, but nothing came out. He glanced down at the picture in her hand. It was a close-up photo of Shanna holding a small baby, its tiny cheek against hers.

For a moment he couldn't do a thing but stare, feeling a strange whirl of emotions—confusion, surprise, fear. And in that instant, Shanna got to her feet, slipped past him into the house.

"Shanna, wait!"

"I'm fine," she said over her shoulder, her voice thick. For a moment he considered going after her, then decided against it. He sat down in one of the creaky rattan chairs, leaned back and rubbed his face.

The image of the picture floated through his mind, Shanna with a baby in her arms, her face full of tenderness, her eyes full of love.

Why had she been crying? He felt a terrible dread creep through his blood. Was this her baby? Where was it? The scenarios that presented themselves were unsettling and he pushed the thoughts away impatiently, got up and poured himself a drink.

It did not escape him how little he knew about this

woman, her past, her life, the people in it. Bright, sunny Shanna—what were her secrets?

Kamau had delayed dinner, waiting for him to return and as they sat down to eat, Shanna was her normal self again. Full of questions, interested, asking about the missing calves. Asking about his father.

He didn't want to talk about his father. What was it with women that they always wanted to know about the past, about what was dead and gone?

The calves were not found that night.

All the next day, driving around the ranch, checking on his various herds, talking to the *wachungai,* Rand kept seeing Shanna in his mind. Thinking of Shanna with a baby in her arms was an oddly confusing thought. Not long ago the image he'd had of her had been all but motherly, and now he didn't know what to think. But the image kept floating through his mind and the uneasy fear that went with it kept stirring his need to know. Where was this baby? Why had she been crying?

For the last few days he had been telling himself not to get drawn into her world, not to start something that would surely end in disaster. There was no future in a relationship with Shanna, he knew well enough. It didn't matter what he felt about her.

He had done nothing but call himself a fool for having asked her to move in. Reasons and excuses enough, but he should have known better. And to top it all off, he had kissed her. What had he been thinking?

The problem was that he had not been. At least not with the intelligent, rational part of his brain.

He'd been feeling, instead of thinking. Feeling her warmth inches away from him, breathing in her fresh, soapy scent; hearing the sound of her voice, soft and sexy in the night air. All his senses had been acutely aware of her standing there in her thin robe with the moonlight silvering her hair, thick, luscious hair he had ached to touch.

He had ached to touch more than just her hair and he'd not been able to resist the temptation.

And now she was here, in his house, in his life and there was no way that with good grace he could retract his invitation and ask her to leave.

And with every smile, every laugh, she crept deeper into his heart. And now she was crying. And somewhere there was a baby, and he did not want to know about it, about her, about her life.

In the distance he saw the tell-tale sign of death—a flock of vultures circling slowly above what most certainly was the carcass of an animal.

"Who cooked this?" Rand wanted to know, looking down at his plate. "Kamau?"

"I did," Shanna said. It was quite a colorful assembly of food—chicken with a spicy ginger sauce with orange mangoes, red and green pepper, yellow lemon wedges. A veritable painter's pallette. Playing with food, she loved it. And today the cooking spirit had moved her and she'd managed to charm Kamau into giving her his kitchen. He'd watched her suspiciously, and Catherine too had joined them, offering to help.

"I should have guessed."

"Why?"

"The colors, for one." He began to eat. "And the spiciness. Definitely you—colorful and spicy."

She laughed, surprised a little at his lighthearted comment. "I hope you like spicy." She heard herself say the words, and groaned inwardly. "Spicy food, I mean," she added, making it worse.

He gave her a quick, amused glance. "I like spicy," he said ambiguously.

"So do I," she returned. He could make of that what he wanted.

"You enjoy cooking?" he asked blandly.

"Yes, as long as I can be creative, use exotic ingredients, you know, experiment a little."

He looked up and there was no denying the devilish glint in his eyes, and she felt a rush of silly embarrassment.

"I am talking about cooking," she said coolly, offering him a haughty look.

"Of course," he said, deadpan, giving his full attention again to the food on his plate.

She took a swallow of wine and decided she'd better watch her words a tad more closely.

"Kamau wasn't too sure he should let me take charge of dinner tonight," she said. "Afraid this sort of thing would be not to your taste, which of course would be a calamity."

He raised his brows at her and kept eating.

"I told him I'd take full responsibility in case you'd fire him," she added solemnly.

He wiped his mouth and lifted his wineglass. "I'm sure he's terribly worried about that eventuality, after thirty years or so."

"That's a long time in the same job." Thirty years ago she hadn't even been born yet, and Kamau had been here, in the same kitchen, cooking Boeuf Bourguignonne.

"Indeed. And if you feel inclined to teach him a few new tricks, please feel free. A little change in the fare around here would be good."

"He's a very good cook," she said truthfully, feeling the need to defend the kind Kamau.

"But his repertoire is not extensive and it's been the same, more or less, for as long as I can remember."

Rand's mother had taught him how to cook. Shanna had seen some of her handwriting in the cookbooks in the kitchen and on some old and faded scraps of paper Kamau had filed away like treasures. Bold, confident handwriting. After all these years Kamau was still making the dishes she'd taught him, unchanged. And when visitors were expected, he baked chocolate-chip cookies.

"Do you miss your mother?" she asked, surprised at herself for asking the question so abruptly.

He did not look up from his plate. "No," he said.

He'd only been a young boy, twenty-some years ago. It was a long time. Still, she felt a strange uneasiness at his cool, terse answer. She took a sip of wine.

"Do you remember much of her, from when you were little?"

"No. I don't spend much time pondering the past." He drained his glass and put his napkin next to his plate, a clear indication he was finished with his meal as well as with the conversation. Shanna pretended not to notice.

"I just mean, you know, did she read you stories? Did she sing songs with you? That sort of thing."

"I assume she did." He pushed his chair back and came to his feet. "This was excellent, thank you. And if you'll excuse me, I have some work to do in my study."

His lust for spice had apparently reached its limits for the day.

She felt dismissed and she didn't like it.

Antonia called in the middle of the next morning. "How do you like the house?" she asked. "Isn't it perfect?"

It took Shanna a second to remember what Antonia was talking about, the thought of her moving to town already history in her mind.

"Yes, perfect," she said truthfully. "But Rand suggested I stay here for the time being. It seems Kamau likes me."

Antonia gave a smothered laugh. "Sure."

"He wants me to teach him to cook some different dishes,

add to his repertoire.'' She didn't know why she was saying this stuff, as if she'd fool anybody.

''Darling,'' Antonia was saying in a long-suffering voice, ''we need to talk.''

''About what?''

Antonia sighed. ''You know about what. You strike me as a perfectly intelligent person.''

''Thank you,'' said Shanna.

''I know you don't want to hear this. I know I should mind my own business. I know Rand is—''

''You know a lot.''

''Yes, I do. Unfortunately. And as a woman, I feel it is my sisterly duty to warn you. He is a very handsome male specimen, Rand is.''

''I am aware of that.''

''And he oozes sex appeal.''

''I've noticed.''

''And he breaks hearts. I don't think he does it on purpose, mind you, it just always seems to turn out that way.''

''So I've heard.''

''Of course, I should have known. It never takes long around here. So you know about Marina.'' It was a statement not a question.

''Yes.'' Well, some. Enough. ''Are you one of his victims, too?''

Antonia laughed. ''Of course, but ages ago, when I was all but nineteen and I'm quite healed, thank you. I just like to give him a bad time about it. We've known each other our whole lives, you know,'' she added wistfully.

''Well,'' Shanna said lightly, ''I do appreciate your concern, but I can take care of myself.''

''Let's hope so,'' Antonia said darkly. ''Now, you're coming to the party, too, on Saturday, aren't you?''

''Yes, if the invitation still stands.''

"Of course it does. And since you'll be flying in with Rand you're spending the night. You're sharing a room?"

The question took her aback. "No," she said. "I hope that's not a problem?"

Antonia laughed. "There's no need to be discreet or anything. Nobody cares."

"I care."

"You have my unmitigated admiration," said Antonia, her tone humorous. "I'll see you two sometime Saturday afternoon, okay?"

"I'm looking forward to it." And she did.

Maybe she'd wear the red dress.

Two more days went by and Shanna had had enough of Rand's remote behavior. If he didn't want her here, she was leaving.

Simple.

When dinner was over and Rand once more excused himself to go hide in his study, Shanna gathered up her courage and decided now was the time. She stood up and followed him down the hall to his study.

"Rand, wait a minute."

He stopped, his hand on the door to his study and turned to her. "Yes?"

"I want to ask you a question," she said, feeling her heart rate speed up in trepidation.

He opened the door and gestured for her to precede him in. "What is it?"

She stood in the middle of the small room and faced him squarely. "I keep getting the feeling you don't want me here," she said, opting for directness.

His brows shot up as if she'd caught him off guard with her question.

"I invited you," he said, putting his hands into his pockets.

"So you did. But I'm wondering if, really, you're sorry now you asked me to stay." She crossed her arms in front of her chest, holding on to herself as if she needed to defend herself against an impending danger. "Is there something I said, or did?" She couldn't imagine what it was.

He frowned. "No, why?"

"You've been giving me mixed signals and it...confuses me. You said you liked my company, you kissed me, and now you're avoiding me. It's like you're trying on purpose not to be with me in the same room. If you changed your mind, and you don't want me around, I want you to tell me. I can leave. It's not a problem." She sounded so business-like, so calm. She felt none of these things. Her heart was racing, her hands clenched so tight, they hurt. "I don't like the feeling that I'm in your way."

"You're not in my way," he said, and he looked suddenly tired, as if weighed down by some invisible burden.

She bit her lip. "Something is going on between us," she said on a low note. "But I don't understand the way you act, as if you're trying to deny it. Is there a problem? I mean, if there is a reason why we shouldn't...be together, I'll leave."

"I don't want you to leave." He reached out and touched her hair and her heart turned over.

"What *do* you want?" she asked.

His face grew still, his eyes filled with shadows. "I want my personal life simple and uncomplicated."

She looked into his eyes. "So do I."

They stood there, the tension mounting, almost touching. Almost.

Then she leaned closer, just a little, stood on tiptoe and very softly put her lips against his. "This is very simple," she whispered, feeling the blood rush through her hot and fast, her heart pounding with her daring.

He reached up with both hands and tunneled his fingers through her hair.

"Are you sure?" he asked

"Yes," she said. "It's simple, what I feel, what I want."

Why should it not be? she wondered. She was drawn to this man with his eyes as blue as the Kenyan sky, with his quiet manner, his competence and strength, his love for his land and the animals in it.

What was wrong in wanting to be closer, to open herself up to him, to fall in love?

His arms came around her and his mouth closed over hers and she felt enveloped, taken in, gathered up with such need and sweetness, her body melted, yielded into his. Her mouth opened, invited, and the kiss grew deeper, more intense. Her head was spinning with the pure wonder of that kiss, the erotic tenderness, the taste of him.

How long this went on, she had no idea. Time danced away into space, her thoughts nothing more than wisps of consciousness. *I want you...you make me feel...please... more, more.*

He released her abruptly, and she felt herself reeling with the suddenness of it. The next thing she knew Catherine, pretty in pink, stood in the open door.

It was a sobering sight. She folded her arms and tried to stop herself from trembling. Where had the girl come from so suddenly? She hadn't heard her approach, but Rand obviously had. The ear of a hunter was a useful tool and Shanna wondered dizzily if it might not be a good idea to start developing one of her own.

Oh," Catherine said, surprised to find Shanna there. "*Memsab,* your coffee is in the sitting room. Shall I bring it here?"

Shanna shook her head. "No, thank you. I'll have it there."

It had always seemed to Shanna that having a staff to do

the cleaning and the washing and the ironing was the ultimate luxury. Clearly this ultimate luxury had its drawbacks. For one, it was interfering in her love life, budding as it was, and this was not a good thing.

Catherine left, closing the door behind her.

The next moment Rand had drawn her back into his arms and was kissing her again with a hungry intensity that sent her senses spinning.

There was nothing tentative about that kiss. It was hot and passionate and impatient.

"What I want," he said against her mouth, "is you. I want you. I want you in my bed. I want to make love to you and I want it so much it scares the hell out of me."

Her heart leaped into her throat. "Why does that scare you?" she whispered, tilting her head back so she could see his face.

"Because I don't know how simple this is...or...will be." He paused. "And I don't want you to get hurt, in the end."

Love was a risk, a leap of faith. It always was, and she knew that well enough.

"I'm not asking for guarantees, Rand."

His hands slipped down her back to her waist. "I know. I still don't want you to get hurt."

"If I get hurt, I'll take responsibility for it," she said. "I am here with you out of my own free will. I can leave anytime I don't want to be with you anymore."

She searched his face, and saw a glimmer of a smile tug a the corner of his mouth. He reached up and stroked her cheek, his fingertips trailing down to caress her lips.

"You sound so brave," he said quietly.

She felt relief at his smile. She smiled back. "I'm very brave," she acknowledged, and Lynn's words flashed like warning flares through her thoughts. "You have no idea how brave," she added, willing away all ominous thoughts.

He framed her face with his hands and kissed her softly. "Come with me," he said.

CHAPTER SEVEN

His study had once been a nursery, she realized, as he led her through the connecting door to his bedroom. One small lamp was on near the bed.

They faced each other silently. The air throbbed around them, filled with an expectant energy that she could feel on her skin like a touch. Her heart beat feverishly, her body trembled. And she knew that if she wanted to change her mind, she'd have to do it now.

She didn't want to change her mind. Every part of her had longed for this moment, longed for him to want her.

And he wanted her.

He did not speak as he began to undress her, kissing her shoulder, her breasts, her belly as he went along, a wonderful sexy game of exploration that made her blood rush wildly through her body. Then she was completely naked before him, her legs barely holding her up.

For a moment the age-old feminine insecurity swept through her. What if he didn't like what he saw? What if he thought her hips were too wide or her breasts...

He was looking at her, his eyes full of blue smoky desire and all doubt was swallowed up. She reached out to unbutton his shirt, but his hands were there first, moving quickly. He was out of his clothes in a flash of time and then he, too, was naked. And he was beautiful, as she had known he would be, all virile male strength and sexual promise. Adam in Paradise.

His face was dark and smoldering as he drew her to him, holding her tight against him. The feeling of his hot, muscled body against her own made her sigh with wonder and desire.

95

"Oh," she whispered, "you feel so good."

He laughed softly, and moved her over to the bed. "It'll get better yet."

She felt the bed beneath her, his body still against hers, his mouth on hers, his tongue seducing hers in a sensuous dance of intimacy.

Her body trembled beneath his. She had known it would happen, known it was inevitable to find herself in his arms, in his bed. It was good, it was right. She wanted him, all of him.

Her body ached for him, as it had for days now. In the dim light of the room, with the sounds from the bush floating in through the open window, his hands searched her body, finding all the secret places, making her nerves sing.

His hands touching, stroking.

His mouth and tongue playing, seducing.

Long, slow, tantalizing touches.

Her body throbbed. Her blood pounded. She gave back, needing to touch him and taste him and make him part of her.

He whispered her name, his voice low and full of yearning and she took it in, the sound of it, like sweet wine. Joy, desire, and a glorious wildness flooded her, an intensity of feeling so overpowering it took her breath away. She let the fire come, let it sweep through her, gave herself up to it.

"Shanna…" he said again, his voice almost a plea. For what, she was not sure.

"Yes," she whispered, saying yes to whatever he needed, wanted, because she wanted nothing more than to love him, chase away the ghosts that haunted him.

She felt the world spin away, was aware only of this moment that was full of him, of his scent, the heat of his kisses. Their bodies tangled in a feverish trance, the need sweeping higher and higher, swirling faster and faster until there was no breath left.

Nothing but the shattering of the trance, the loss of all control. Oblivion.

They did not speak for a long time.

Motionless, spent, they lay together while reality slowly spun back into the room, sounds from outside floating in on the breeze.

Slowly, as consciousness returned, Shanna stirred and sighed, hearing the wind in the trees, the vibrating chorus of the insects. Her eyes still closed, she snuggled closer. She felt a delicious lassitude, the aftermath of lovemaking, but she wasn't ready for sleep. It was only just after nine in the evening.

"Rand?" she whispered.

"Yes."

"Are you going to sleep?"

He gave a soft laugh. "No. I'm just recuperating."

"You know what I'd like?"

He groaned. "I'm not fifteen."

She laughed. "I want some of that chocolate cake Kamau made. And coffee with some brandy in it."

"Good idea." He raised himself on one elbow. "And Shanna?" His voice was low, filled with softness.

"Yes?"

"Don't go back to your own room tonight." With his free hand he brushed her tangled hair away from her face. "Unless you want to."

Her heart filled with sweetness. "I don't want to."

"See the blond one?" Antonia asked, pointing at a large framed photograph on the wall. "That's Rand's mother."

Party noises cheerfully danced around them—people laughing, the sounds of ice clinking against glass, music. Antonia's house was large and airy and now full of people who'd driven and flown in for the festivities.

It had been the first time ever Shanna had flown in a tiny

airplane, a Cessna, and she'd had to admit to being terrified at first, even with Rand at the controls next to her, radiating calm competence. She'd felt totally vulnerable in the tiny plane which on the inside seemed hardly bigger than a car. But once in the air, when her poor pounding heart had dropped out of her throat to its proper position in her chest, she began to feel the exhilarating sense of freedom as they floated across the magnificent landscape below.

Antonia was showing her a collection of photographs displayed along a wall in the hallway, one featuring a group of people, a dead leopard, a blond woman carrying a gun. Rand's mother.

"Did she shoot the leopard?" Shanna asked.

Antonia nodded. "Poachers had wounded it. It had to be shot." She sighed. "Such a waste."

"Did you know her?"

"When I was little, yes. I'd stay with them sometimes, when my parents were away. She was fun. She'd play the piano and we'd make up silly songs. Or she'd teach us how to dance."

Antonia's father joined them. He had thick gray hair and the rugged, handsome face of a man who'd spent his life outdoors. He looked at the photo of Rand's mother. "Gregarious, vivacious woman," he acknowledged with a smile. "Loved a good party." He shook his head regretfully. "We all missed her when she left."

"When she left?" Shanna asked, surprised.

He frowned. "Yes, a long time ago."

"Oh, I...I thought she had died." Why had she assumed that? She couldn't remember what Nick had said and Rand certainly hadn't told her.

"What...why did she leave?"

He shrugged. "Who knows? She simply left and went back to America one day. Lots of stories, but I'm not certain anyone knows the truth."

Shanna stared at the photo, at the smiling woman. "She was...is beautiful," she said, her mind suddenly crowded with a hundred questions.

"Yes." He smiled at Shanna appreciatively. "Blond, with green eyes, like you."

Someone pressed a glass of wine in her hand, drew her attention to one of the other photographs and she was lost in other stories about safari adventures. More people—smiling, asking her questions. Was she new in the country? What was she doing here? Where was she living?

Rand could see the women were sizing her up—a popular party game: dissection and analysis of the new *wazungu* arrivals on the scene. They came and went in this country, lured by the adventure, the romance, the mystique of Africa. The unspoken questions were always the same and he could see them in their faces as they talked to Shanna. Would she be an interesting or amusing addition to their dinner parties? Competition on the sexual scene? Would she sleep with their husbands? This outwardly sophisticated, cosmopolitan tribe was at heart nothing but a troop of provincial busybodies. He watched Shanna as she talked, wondering if he should come to the rescue.

Not necessary. She was quite aware of what was going on, not fazed at all, he could tell just looking at her expression and the way she held herself.

Smart girl, he thought. She was no one's fool in her red dress. It was quite stunning in its elegant simplicity, yet daring of color, an interesting combination to be worn by this smiling woman with her open, fresh face. This woman he'd made love to last night, who'd slept in his arms.

He looked at her standing there in her red dress, smiling at the women, looking perfectly at ease. She was all feminine softness and sexy vibrancy, but he'd recognized the strong core in her, a depth of passion and personal integrity that would keep her standing in a storm.

She was full of contradiction and surprises.

He was suddenly overwhelmed by the need to hold her, take her away from all these people, have her to himself, warm himself with her presence, the sound of her voice.

Shanna was enjoying herself. After several weeks of solitary toil on her father's book, she was ready for a little frivolity. Even Rand seemed to enjoy himself, which was a good sign. He was talking to Antonia's husband, talking ranching business, no doubt, but still he looked relaxed.

"So," said Lynn, materializing next to her with a drink in her hand. "You, too, huh? Smitten, I can see."

"Everybody knows everything around here, it seems," Shanna said, trying not to show her irritation.

Lynn laughed. "All I have to do is look at your face when you watch him."

"Really?" She tried to sound bored. Why couldn't people mind their own business? She liked Lynn well enough, but she wasn't ready to share her innermost feelings with her just yet.

"I just hope you're not going into this blindly."

"Me, too," said Shanna.

Lynn stared at her, then sighed. "Just don't get yourself too emotionally invested or you'll get hurt."

"I will try not to."

Emotionally invested? Shanna asked herself. Is that what's happening to me? And how did you *not* get emotionally invested when falling hopelessly in love? Last night had been wonderful. Rand had been wonderful—passionate, caring.

Lynn gave an apologetic little shrug. "I don't mean to be the High Priestess of Doom, but I know what Marina went through, and it wasn't pretty."

Shanna didn't want to hear any more about the poor suffering Marina, so she changed the subject, which was just as well because Rand appeared by her side a moment later.

"Hello, Lynn," he said smoothly.

Lynn glowered at him. "Hello, Rand." Her voice was coolly polite.

He turned to Shanna. "Antonia is showing her film in the library. She wonders if you're interested."

"Oh, of course! I'd love to."

They sat in the dark room, watching the film about the tribal customs of the Samburu. Rand had his arm around her, and she leaned her head against his shoulder, feeling happy, as she watched the colorful ceremony on the screen.

"Do you want to sleep alone tonight?" he whispered in her ear.

They'd each been given a room, as requested, but they were next to each other, probably not by coincidence; Antonia hadn't believed for a minute she'd wanted to sleep alone.

It was a straightforward question and she didn't feel like being coy or playing games.

"No," she said.

He kissed her neck, and she felt his smile against her skin. "You don't want to play hard to get?"

"No. You might take me seriously."

He laughed softly. "I like you better all the time."

Warmth washed over her and she snuggled closer in the dark room as the images flitted across the screen, feeling gloriously in love.

Well, she was.

Gloriously emotionally invested, so to speak.

The Monday after the party, Shanna drove to Rosemary's house and found the door open, the screen door letting in the cool morning air.

"Rosemary!" she called out. "Are you there?"

"Yes! Come in," came a voice from somewhere in the house. Shanna opened the screen door and stepped into the living room.

"I'm in the bathroom!" Rosemary called out. "Come on, give me a hand."

This seemed a rather strange request, but Shanna rushed into the hallway and found the bathroom door open and Rosemary squashed between the wall and the toilet, with her head nearly into the open water tank.

"What are you *doing?*" Shanna asked, watching this strange sight.

Rosemary lifted her face and gave a frustrated grunt. "The wretched thing is broken again and I'm trying to fix it." She glanced down again and resumed her fiddling with the mechanisms in the tank.

Shanna knew enough not to suggest she call a plumber.

"Can I help?" she said instead, which was just as useless an idea. She laughed at herself. "Not that I know anything about this sort of thing."

"You can give me that piece of wire over there."

Shanna did as requested, watching with admiration as Rosemary twisted and manipulated the metal and did something mysterious with it inside the tank. Finally she struggled out from her narrow space and flipped the handle. The tank flushed, making all the appropriate noises.

"I'm impressed," Shanna said. "You fixed it."

"For as long as it lasts. Come on, I need a coffee."

A week earlier she had caught Rosemary taking apart a water faucet and fix it. "How do you know all this stuff?"

Rosemary shrugged. "Here, in the bush, you'd better learn."

She liked Rosemary's easy competence, and surprised herself with the sudden wish to be more like that as well. A little mechanical ability in a place like this would certainly be useful. Unfortunately, she had none.

Well, she could learn. Somehow. She thought of Antonia flying her own plane, of Rand's mother shooting a leopard. Helpless females were not a breed that would survive for long in the bush, and she wanted to survive. She did not want to feel helpless or incompetent.

And why, she asked herself, is this suddenly so important?

"Have a seat," Rosemary said, waving in the direction of the sitting room. "I'll wash up and tell Moses to bring us some coffee."

In the sitting room Shanna's attention was drawn to a colorful painting on the wall. She'd seen it before, but hadn't studied it up close; it wasn't that kind of painting. Why she did now, she didn't know. Close up the images blurred in splashes of formless color. Only the artist's signature was now in focus: Marina Summers.

Her heart lurched at seeing the name.

She stepped back, looked at the colorful, impressionistic painting with a new eyes. A scene straight out of the Garden of Eden, a lush landscape, a waterfall, all God's creatures drinking at a water hole. And on an outcropping high up, two small human figures, a man and a woman, standing close together surveying the panoramic view.

Marina had made this painting, the canvas reflecting her feelings, the stirrings of her soul. Shanna felt a strange lightness, as if some great truth suddenly became clear to her. As if this Marina was no longer just a name, a faceless person hidden in the shadows of other people's memories.

Marina was a real person, and she had lived with Rand, had loved him, slept with him. And she had loved this land and seen its beauty, idealized it, no doubt. Shanna stared at the painting, and suddenly noticed something else.

In the lower left corner, below the rocky outcropping lay a pile of animal bones, dried and bleached in the sun.

There was no perfection, not even in Paradise, and Marina had known that, too. There were many tragedies, danger, death, lost love.

Lost love.

Like a gust of cold wind, fear swept through her.

Shanna turned away abruptly and sat down in a chair facing the opposite wall which was covered floor-to-ceiling with shelves full of books, a more calming view for the moment. She did not want to think about Marina.

Rosemary rescued her from her thoughts. "Did you bring me your manuscript?" she asked.

"The first few chapters," she said.

Rosemary had offered to read the manuscript, help out with editing or advise. Having grown up in the country, she might spot mistakes and inconsistencies.

"You don't know how glad I am you're willing to do this, you know. Have somebody look at it with a fresh eye is so important."

"I'm looking forward to it, actually," Rosemary said. "Something a bit more cerebral than what I spend most of my time doing." She grimaced. "Office work, dispensing aspirin, repairing toilets."

Later, as Shanna drove back to the ranch house, she thought of the painting, of Marina. Where was she now? What did she look like? Would she one day run into her, at a party?

"Bwana! Bwana! Look!" Shrieking in delighted terror, a group of village children surrounded Rand as he jumped out of his Land Rover. One little girl, eight or nine, had her baby sister tied on her back.

Babies; he was seeing them everywhere. Where had they all come from so suddenly during the last week?

One boy stood apart from the rest, the others apparently too frightened to come near him. Kamau's grandson, Rand saw. The kid was the biggest of the little gang, with huge eyes and a cocky, fearless grin. As he came toward Rand, the other children moved away. He held out his cupped hands to show Rand his scary treasure: a chameleon.

By human standards of beauty it was a repulsive little creature, looking quite prehistoric with its rough, blistery skin, big toothless mouth, and large protruding, swiveling eyes. Feared by many of the local people for mythical and mystical reasons, the chameleon was usually left alone and the bravery of the boy was quite impressive. It also did not bode well for the little reptile's fate.

Rand admired it, giving his usual speech about being gentle, about not hurting innocent animals, about respecting nature.

Unless nature didn't respect you, of course.

He tried to persuade the boy to let the harmless creature go, knowing it was useless. They would play with it, endlessly, innocently, and the tiny dinosaur look-alike might not find it so entertaining.

Fortunately, the chameleon was spared this playing session when the boy's mother came on the scene and had a fit, shrieking about the perils and evils that would befall the kid if he did not immediately let go of it.

"I'll take it," said Rand, and the boy reluctantly handed it over.

The woman grabbed her son by his Superman T-shirt and hauled him away. The baby on her back slept peacefully on, oblivious of the noise and commotion.

Rand had never realized how many babies there were. Ever since he'd seen the photo of Shanna with the baby, they had appeared from nowhere, or so it seemed.

She had not mentioned the baby and he had not asked. He was a coward, he knew, and he did not like himself for it.

He went inside the office and deposited the chameleon in the plant on Rosemary's desk.

"Why, thank you," she said, "I so love pretty presents."

"Don't mention it."

"Was that what all the commotion was about outside?"

"Yes. Don't let them get him again. Take him home and put him in your garden or something."

"Why don't you take him home? Give him to Shanna. She'll love him."

"Probably. She loves baboons, too."

He found himself smiling as he went into his office. Until he looked outside his window and saw the wife of the office *askari* strolling by, with a baby on her back.

"Rand?"

He turned, seeing Rosemary standing in the door with the chameleon on her shoulder.

"Yes?"

"About Shanna…" Rosemary hesitated.

"What about Shanna?" He didn't like the sound of this. He didn't want to discuss Shanna. "You're reading her manuscript," he said, a blatant diversion technique.

"Yes. She gave it to me yesterday and I started it last night. It's really good, but that's not what I wanted to talk about." She bit her lip, fixing him with an intense dark gaze. She was not going to get sidetracked, he could tell.

"Please, Rand," she said in a low tone, "don't screw it up this time, will you?"

This was not what he wanted to hear, and he was aware she knew it. He gave her a cool look and was just about to say something about her minding her own business when she held up her hand to stop him.

"Don't say a thing," she said. "You're coming through loud and clear without it."

Don't screw it up this time. To his great exasperation, the words kept echoing in his mind for the rest of the day.

Was he in the process of making another monumental mistake? He thought of Marina and the guilt washed over him again. He had not loved her, at least he had never allowed himself to believe he had. And now, here was another woman in his house, one he wanted so much it was driving him crazy.

He did not know if he loved her. He did not know if he was capable of love at all.

It was not a happy thought.

CHAPTER EIGHT

It was quite a view that greeted him when Rand drove up to the house that night.

A shapely bottom in khaki shorts above smooth bare legs caught his immediate attention. The rest of the female figure was bent over underneath the raised hood of an old Land Rover, apparently engrossed in the mechanisms hiding there.

He jumped out of his car and moved in for a closer look. "Shanna?"

"Yeah," she muttered, then raised her head and glanced at him over her shoulder. "Hi."

"*What* are you doing?"

She grinned. "I'm bonding with my car." She had a book in her left hand and she waved it at him. "'Car Repair for the Mechanically Challenged,'" she added for clarification.

"This...car is yours?"

"Yep. I just bought it this morning."

Looking at the heap of junk, he was not encouraged by this news. "And it's causing problems already?"

She straightened up and looked at him fully. "Oh, no, I am just trying to figure out what's what. Getting the lay of the land, so to speak. It seems like I should know some basics, like where the battery is and such. And how to change a tire, you know."

He almost laughed. "You don't know how to change a tire?"

"Never learned, no. You know, me, a city girl and all. Repair shops never far and helpful people everywhere, and taxis in abundance if all else fails."

"And why this sudden enthusiasm?"

108

She tossed her hair back and pulled her shirt down. She looked too damned sexy for her own good, her breasts full and round under the pink cotton. She shaded her eyes against the brilliant sunlight. "Well, I live in darkest Africa now," she said wryly, "and it seems that the physical environment necessitates a certain amount of mechanical competence. I wouldn't want to get stuck here in the bush with a broken-down car with all these wild animals all around waiting to pounce and make dinner out of me. Which reminds me, I would like to learn how to use a gun."

He wasn't sure he heard right.

She frowned. "You're staring. Is that bad or weird?"

"No, no, of course not. I just hadn't thought you the type."

She rolled her eyes. "Like I'm too delicate or something? Listen, I just want to be practical, that's all. I have no blood-thirsty motives. I don't want to kill anything just for the fun of it. I just want to be safe when I go out. Like you and everybody else around here."

"You can take one of the *askaris* with you."

"I don't want to feel so dependent, Rand. Really, I want to be able to take care of myself."

Determined, sincere. "There's more involved than just shooting a riffle. You've got to know what to look and listen for, what the danger signs are…" He shook his head, how did one teach a savvy urbanite how to be a competent bush woman?

She sighed. "Rand, I know. I was only a kid when I lived here, but I'm not stupid. I know with you it's inbred. You grew up here, you know every blade of grass and every smell and every sound of this place, and I'll never know all that, but I know a few things and I can learn more, and I can practice. If you'll teach me."

She amazed him, this woman. How could he possibly refuse?

"All right," he said. "I'll teach you."

She gave him a happy grin. "Great. When can we start? Saturday?"

"If you like."

She turned back to the car, reached up and slammed the hood closed. She leaned her hip against the fender and gave the damn thing a possessive slap.

"So, what do you think?"

It was a battered four-wheel drive, army green, an old workhorse ready for pasture. He feared for what lurked beneath its ugly body.

"Cool, right?" she asked, her eyes glimmering with humor, daring him to contradict her.

"Only if it doesn't disintegrate on you. Where did you buy it? Who sold it to you?"

She gave him a disparaging look. "You don't think I know how to buy a car?"

In light of what she had just told him about her mechanical competence, no, not for a minute. "I am not sure," he lied. "So, where did you find this relic?"

"I bought it from someone in Nyahururu." Her eyes were laughing and he knew she was enjoying his suspicions. "A friend of Bengt's, you know the Swedish volunteer who lives in my old house in Kanguli. I met him a couple of weeks ago and I mentioned to him I wanted a car and it so happens that he himself is a serious car nut and he found this one for me. He more or less took it apart to make sure it's okay, and he even fixed some things for me. He knows somebody who has a car repair shop."

She sure made friends in a fast hurry, he thought a bit sourly. "And you trust this Bengt?"

"Yes, I do, of course." She tilted her head a little. "My instincts about people are pretty good, you know. If they're not to be trusted, I get this weird feeling here." She poked herself in the solar plexus. Then she gave him another dazzling smile. "So, do you approve?"

He wondered why it mattered, but he enjoyed her enthusiasm and couldn't help putting his arm around her and kiss her on the cheek. Which was a rather sedate expression of what he really felt like doing right here and now.

"As long as it's safe to drive," he said, leading her into the house, planning to make sure it was the case for his own peace of mind.

"Oh, I'm sure it is."

He took her into the bedroom, locked the door and began pulling her shirt out of the waistband of her shorts.

"What are you doing?" she asked, laughing, trying to wriggle free, but not trying really hard.

"I am taking off your clothes and after that I will take off mine. And then I want you to do something for me."

"I'm not sure I want to," she said primly.

"You'll want to, trust me."

"You're very sure of yourself, aren't you?"

He gave her a devilish grin. "Yes, I am."

"And what exactly is it that you want me to do for you?"

"I want you to get into the shower with me and give me a very thorough soapy massage."

"Only if you give me one, too," she said.

He had to ask.

He could not go on not knowing.

Bracing himself mentally, Rand sat down next to Shanna on the sofa. She was pouring their after-dinner coffee and he watched her for a moment as she performed the simple task. He liked looking at her. Even if all she did was pour coffee. Or walk across the lawn. Or read. Or butter a piece of bread.

He took the cup she handed him. "There's something I

want to ask you,'' he said, knowing he was going where he didn't want to go, feeling compelled to do it anyway.

"Okay.'' She looked at him, her eyes a translucent green.

"Last week one night when I came home I found you crying. Why?''

She glanced away, at the dogs lying by the fire. "I was just…I was just in a sentimental mood, that's all.''

"I saw the picture you had in your hand,'' he said.

"Oh.'' She was silent for a moment, apparently digesting this. "He's not my baby, if you were wondering.''

It was like a weight had been lifted from his heart. "He's not?''

"Is that what you were thinking?'' She frowned. "Well, I suppose that's what it looked like.''

"I kept wondering what might have happened.''

"Oh.'' Her eyes widened in horror. "I'm sorry! I didn't realize you'd seen the picture and what you might be thinking…I'm sorry.''

"It's all right. But why were you crying?''

"I miss him. I took care of him for over ten months and I miss him and sometimes it's hard to look at a picture without getting emotional about it.''

"Whose baby was it? Why were you taking care of it?''

"Mostly, it was because of a terrible bureaucratic tangle. It's a long story.'' She hesitated. "You want to me to tell you?''

He had started it. He could not now say he didn't want to hear her story. He nodded.

"I have a good friend who's a social worker with an adoption agency and one day I went to her office—I forget why—and I found her in the middle of a crisis with this baby. He was right there with her, in her office, sleeping in a car seat. He was supposed to be handed over to adoptive parents and something terrible had happened, a bad accident, and they couldn't take him anymore. It was a few days before Christmas, and my friend was about to drop with a horrible case of the flu and she'd spent hours trying to locate a foster home for the baby and everybody in the system had either a house full of guests or was in bed with the flu, and well, to make a long story short, I took him home with me.''

"You took a strange baby home with you, just like that?''

She smiled crookedly. "It seemed like the sensible thing to do under the circumstances, but it was probably against all the rules and laws of the land. But my friend was about to keel over and was only too glad to have found a responsible solution, whatever the rules.''

"How old was he?''

"Ten days. A newborn, straight from the hospital.''

"I expect you were not exactly prepared to have a baby in your house.''

She laughed. "No. I remember driving home with him in his car seat and thinking, *Oh, my God, what did I do!* But my neighbor had had a baby a few months earlier, and she had everything I needed to get me started, including formula samples she'd never used because she was nursing, and it all worked fine.''

"And they never found a foster home for him? You just kept him?''

"Well, you know how it is with the holidays. By the time it was January I still had him, and then because of all kinds of mishaps and coincidences and bureaucracy tangles, I ended up having him for another month and then they didn't think it was in the baby's interest to move to another temporary place before an adoption was arranged, so I kept him and then it was almost ten months before another adoption was in place. Don't ask me why it took so long. Anyway, by then he was sitting up and crawling and....'' She looked down on her hands.

"By then he was yours and you didn't want to give him up.''

"Right. But he was mine long before that, really. I was his mother, the only one he had ever known, and I loved him with all my heart, even though I knew I could never keep him."

He saw her eyes fill with tears, saw her fight them back. He put his arm around her.

"Ten months is quite a commitment. What about your own life, your work?"

"I was working for a professor doing research and I could do most of that at home and my writing for the university journal I did at home. It really worked out very well. And then I got the contract for my father's book and an advance so I gave up the research job and started working on the draft. I was home with Sammy almost all the time."

She looked away and was silent for a moment and he had no idea what to say, so he just tightened his arm around her.

"And then he was gone," she said softly. "My apartment was so empty, I couldn't stand it. They'd warned me not to get attached too much, but I don't know how you do that. I don't know how you cannot love a baby you've hugged and cuddled and fed and taken care of for so long, even if he's not your own. Even if you know it's temporary and you can't keep him."

Probably inevitable for any woman with all her normal female instincts in play, he thought. And Shanna seemed to have hers in perfect order.

She took a deep breath. "I tried to adopt him myself, but that was out of the question because of all sorts of rules." She looked up at the ceiling, fighting her tears. "So, I had to give him up. It was the most difficult thing I have ever done in my whole life."

"And when was this?"

"A couple of months before I came here." She ran her tongue over her lips. "I'm so happy I could come here, to be away from it all, and because I always wanted to come back. It helps to be in new surroundings with people who don't know about it and to have a job to do that I like so I can keep my mind busy. But still..." She closed her eyes. "Sometimes it just hurts to look at the picture because all I want is to hold him again. I miss just feeling him in my arms, smelling his baby smell. It's purely selfish of me, because he doesn't need me now. He has a perfectly wonderful home with loving parents. Two of them."

"But when he did need you you were there."

And she had given him everything, her love, her care and attention, her time. And now it was no longer needed. He felt an overwhelming tenderness, a deep need to comfort her. It was a novel feeling, this softness inside him.

This woman he had so misjudged kept surprising him more and more. Intruded in his thoughts and dreams more and more, and along with all his feelings of need and desire there was also the deep sense of fear. *It will never last.*

Need and desire were easy. Dealing with the fear was not.

So he pushed the fear away, put his hand on her hair, thick and soft as silk and kissed her. She was here, now. The future was a long way off.

"I did it! I did it!" Shanna leaped into the air, delighted with having hit the target just about dead center. Then she grinned at Rand. "But I'm glad it's just a dead piece of wood and not something alive and breathing."

Never in her life had she expected to find herself in this situation—not only with a gun in her hands, but actually aiming and shooting one. She gave a little shiver, reminding herself that this was necessary for her own safety. Fate was leading her down a new path full of excitement and surprises.

A path with an unknown destiny.

As the weeks went by, Rand taught her how to improve her technique, to recognize animal tracks and how to "read" the landscape. She learned to listen for the sounds—the crackling of twigs, the rustling of leaves. At night the air was filled with the sound of animals—roars, grunts, coughs, barks and whines. Soon, she could identify many of them.

On the mechanical front she was getting an education as well. Rand showed her how to change a tire and enlightened her about some of the other mechanical mysteries of her car. Her life was full of new insights and discoveries. It was interesting and fun.

It was easy.

All she had to do was ask Rand and he would tell her and explain things to her. About the wildlife, the farm, the people who worked for him.

She also discovered what was not easy.

Whenever the subject was himself, Rand wasn't talking. Even the simplest questions went unanswered.

A secret fear began to nestle itself in a dark corner of her heart. She tried not to feel it, think about it.

She spent three days away from the ranch, driving around, looking at the scenery, visiting villages, talking to people, using her impression to get the right feeling for the book. The car held up beautifully. She had a wonderful time and came back full of stories. At night, in bed, she was still talking. Rand listened with interest, asking questions, and she felt a sudden wave of gratitude, knowing he cared about her work, about her feelings and opinions.

''I'm glad I'm home,'' she said, snuggling deeper into his arms.

''Mmm, me, too.''

''Funny,'' she said dreamily, ''to think this feels like home now and a few months ago I had never even been here.''

''Mmm.'' He nibbled her earlobe. ''Don't get too used to it.''

''Why not? I love this place.''

"And a few months from now you'll be gone."

She sighed. "Maybe not. Maybe I'll just stay on, write my own books, become a real bush woman, make love to you a lot. Not a bad life."

He sat up, leaned on one elbow and gave her a crooked smile. "Until you get tired of it and start clamoring for the seductions of the big city."

"Yeah," she said dryly, "the smog, the rat race, apartment life, traffic jams. I can hardly wait."

"You told me Boston is a great city and you loved it."

She faked an innocent look. "Did I say that?"

"Yes, you did."

"I don't remember," she lied.

"Theaters, museums, excellent shopping, gourmet restaurants, the university, a stimulating social life," he enumerated.

"Oh, that," she said laconically.

"Yes, *that*. Give it a couple of months, and you'll be quite anxious to get back to urban civilization."

She put her hands behind her head and looked up at the ceiling. "Oh, well," she said carelessly, "if I do, I'll just get on a plane and leave. Flights every day of the week, easy."

"You're a free woman."

"So I am." She turned on her side and gave him a cheery smile. "Then I'll have to find myself another lover, and that might be interesting. What do you think? A professor of English maybe, or an orthodontist, or—"

He rolled on top of her, silencing her with his mouth. "Shut up," he growled against her lips.

She laughed. "Fortunately, no city stirrings in my soul just yet."

Only the fear, stirring in the darkness.

What if, as with Marina, he would never open up to her? What if it would all go wrong in the end?

She pushed the fear away, reveling in the touch of his mouth, his hands—drifting away into a world where everything felt blissfully right.

"Do you have any pictures of when you were a boy?" she asked him one evening. She'd shown him a picture of her father and herself, a favorite one she kept in her work room, the guest room where at first she had slept.

"Somewhere, yes. Why?"

She shrugged. "Just want to see what you looked like." Strangely, she had trouble imagining him as a little boy, carefree, happy, playing with snakes and chameleons, poking around in the mud. "Don't you have any photo albums?"

"There's a box of photos somewhere, no albums."

No albums. Why no albums? Didn't everybody have at least some sort of family photo album? She kept the thought to herself.

"Would you mind if I had a look at them?"

He shrugged, his face closed, expressionless. "I'll see if I can find them."

It was clear he was not happy with the idea, but could think of no way to refuse her request. He didn't like the idea of her knowing too much, getting too close.

"It's all right, don't worry about it," she said lightly. "Another time maybe."

He met her eyes for a moment. "As you wish."

Later that night she lay in bed, her face against his chest. "Remember Antonia's party?" She didn't know why suddenly she had the need to talk about this, to let him know what she knew.

"What about it?"

"She has a wall full of old safari photos in her house. I'm sure you've seen them. Antonia showed me a picture of your mother, the one with the leopard she shot.'' His body tensed, she was sure she did not imagine it.

She waited but he did not respond.

''I thought she had died,'' she said softly. ''I don't know why I thought that.''

''She didn't,'' he said curtly. ''She left and it's a long time ago. People talk too damn much at these parties.''

''Why don't you ever talk about your mother?'' she asked.

''Because I don't want to.''

''Did you ever see her after she left Kenya?''

''No. And I would appreciate it if you didn't pay any attention to whatever gossip you hear.''

He eased her away from him, got out of bed and stalked to the window. He opened it a little more. ''Will you be too cold?''

Not because of the night air, she wanted to say.

''I'll be fine,'' she said instead, feeling her apprehension grow.

Life was easy and happy as long as she didn't ask him anything very personal, about the past, his mother. And in turn he asked her little about her past life, as if the present was all that mattered—the happiness of the here and now.

He got back into bed, and they lay there, silent.

''I'm sorry if I upset you with my question,'' she said. ''It's just…I miss my own parents, still. I'd do anything if I could have them back.'' She swallowed. ''I wish…I wish I understood you better.''

She felt his hand, reaching out to her in the dark. She took it, held it, and then he moved closer, drew her into his arms and kissed her.

She closed her eyes and gave herself up to it, to him, to her love for him.

His kiss was tender, sweet, at first, moving from her mouth to her chin and throat and breasts. He touched every little part of her, stroking, tasting, taking his time, as if he wanted to commit to memory every little nuance of her body.

She was floating, touching him back, feeling the sweet desire swimming through her, feeling, too, with some separate part of her, a sadness, a strange melancholy in his lovemaking.

Afterward she lay awake while Rand was sleeping next to her.

Making love was the easiest, most natural thing in the world. In bed, she felt close to him, a closeness that had nothing to do with words and memories and things unknown. They belonged together; she felt the truth of it with every cell of her being when she was in his arms.

But sometimes, at odd moments during the day, she'd look at him and feel a vast and gaping void between them, and know something was terribly wrong.

She listened to his breathing and thought of Marina, the woman who had lived with him for a year and the reason that she had left.

And fear rushed in, hot and painful.

No guiding light, no set of instructions. All she had was her own compass and it was twirling crazily, offering no direction.

One evening, to Shanna's happy surprise, Melanie called from Boston.

"Hi, Melanie! Is everything okay?"

"We're all fine here, but I have some news you might want to know. About Tom."

"Tom? Is he all right?" The question came automatically. He had a dangerous job as a police detective.

"He's fine. He got married yesterday."

Tom, married.

"Oh, well, that's good, Melanie. I want him to be happy."

"I know, it's just…well, shoot, I don't know how to tell you this."

"What? Just say it." She had no idea what Melanie could find so hard to say.

"He married a police widow with three young children."

Shanna felt her mouth drop open, her heart skidded. She sat down in a chair.

"Shanna?"

"Yes."

"Are you okay?"

"Yes…I…I don't know what to say."

"There's more." Melanie hesitated. "He's no longer with the police force."

"I don't believe it," she whispered. "Police work is his life."

"The word is he did it for the children."

Shanna took in a deep breath. "For the children," she repeated tonelessly.

"He told you he never wanted kids, Shanna. I don't get it."

"He must have changed his mind." She couldn't think right; her mind a muddle of thoughts and feelings. Of painful memories and difficult choices.

"Are you upset?"

Shanna thought about that. "No. I don't think so. It's behind me. But I'm confused."

"When I heard it I was furious," Melanie admitted. "I kept thinking about you, how hard it all was for you, and then the breakup. And here he is, with three children and…and then you got Sammy and had to give him up and…" Melanie's voice broke. "Oh, damn it, Shanna, you loved that man!"

"Melanie, don't go crying over my past love life!"

Shanna couldn't believe her own light tone. "It's been over for a long time. I'm fine. I'm not having a crisis over Tom changing his mind. I just hope he'll be happy."

"You're a saint," said Melanie. "I would have gone over there and put poison in the wedding cake."

Shanna managed a smile. "Oh, you talk big."

"You look a little shell-shocked," Rand said after she put down the phone. "Shall I pour you a drink?"

"Yes, thank you." Her nerves were a tad shaky, she had to admit.

"Bad news?" he asked her as he handed her a glass of wine.

She shook her head. "No, not really." She hesitated. "You know I told you about Tom a while ago." She hadn't told him any details and he hadn't asked. Just that she had been in a relationship that had ended after four years.

"The police detective?"

"Yes." She took a sip of the wine. "He was married yesterday." And then she told him the story while he listened quietly.

"Now that I think about it, he didn't necessarily change his mind about fathering children," she said finally. "If we'd stayed together he'd still not want to have kids. In the back of his mind he was always worried about something happening and leaving his children fatherless. He never had a father himself."

"But now he has three children."

"Yes." She took the last swallow of wine. "Their father was a policeman. What happened to them was what worried him about having children of his own."

And now, in this strange twist of circumstances he was a father after all. And he had left the police force to protect these children from more possible trauma. And most likely his wife as well.

"Did he ever suggest leaving the force when you were together?" Rand asked.

She gave a small smile. "No, and I never asked him to. He loved his work." She stared into her empty glass. "And I never considered giving up motherhood for our relationship, either," she said quietly.

The room was full of children and Shanna was holding a baby in her arms. The children were all theirs, she told him, and they had just arrived from Boston and they were never going to leave. They all loved the ranch and he was their father and he had to teach them how to hunt and fish. And then his mother walked in and said she'd play the piano and would teach them how to sing.

He could not breathe. The children were crowding around him and he could not breathe. And Shanna was laughing, laughing...

"You can't leave," he managed to say, gasping for air.

"Why not?" she said. "I am a free woman."

"You can't leave," he said again, but his voice was thick and feeble.

"Sure I can," she said. "There're flights out of here every day of the week."

He woke up in a cold sweat, his heart pounding hard against his rib cage.

The room was in darkness. He lay still until his heart calmed down. Then he carefully reached out and found Shanna lying next to him, sound asleep. She didn't stir when he touched her.

Next year, when he reached out, would he still find her next to him?

Rand never knew where he would find her when he came home—on the veranda reading or writing, in the kitchen with Kamau, out in the garden picking flowers, or in front of the bookcases in the living room, surrounded by piles of books looking for some obscure bit of information on Samburu tribal rites or the blooming season of a tree, or the feeding behavior of a particular animal.

He found her in the garden, sitting in an old safari chair in the shade of a yellow fever tree, reading through her father's manuscript, a pencil in her hand. Her hair was pulled up into an untidy knot and curly wisps hung down along her temples. She was so engrossed in her reading, she didn't notice him coming toward her across the lawn.

Her legs were bare, her white shorts held up with a colorful Turkana beaded belt. A glass of something cold stood dripping condensation on a small rattan table by her side.

He watched her, drinking in the sight of her, the color of her hair, the curve of her neck, the shape of her bare feet. Her toenails were painted a frivolous sky blue, which made him smile. He'd not seen that before, wondering what had inspired her to even buy that color, put it on.

She looked up, startled a little as he stood in front of her. Then came the familiar radiant smile, the light coming on in her eyes. She was always so happy to see him.

His insides churned painfully, his heart contracted, and for a moment he fought the impulse to run away, escape from this sticky, silvery web of sweetness and desire.

But he did not. It was too late, much too late.

He bent down and kissed her quickly, smelling the fresh, flowery scent of her hair. "You looked quite engrossed," he said lightly.

"Yeah." Her eyes took on a faraway look, her mind back on her reading. "I've been reading about this old medicine woman my father knew—she knew all about medicinal herbs and plants. I went looking for her, but she died years ago. I wish I knew more." She sighed.

"It's a dying art," he said. "The new generation is interested in computers, not ancient herbal remedies."

"How dare they," she said with a crooked smile. "Oh, by the way, Lynn called me today. She invited me to come down for a few days. She'll show me around Nairobi. We'll do some shopping."

A sudden rush of irritation caught him off guard.

Shanna looked at him, eyes widening in surprise. "What's wrong?"

"Nothing." He pushed his hands in his pockets and produced a smile.

"Don't you like Lynn and Charlie?"

He shrugged. "Charlie is a fool." A singing fool with a red beard.

Shanna laughed. "He has his own way of looking at the world and he does cheer people up with his songs. What about Lynn?"

"Lynn's married to Charlie."

And if that wasn't enough, the woman talked too much, knew too much, had given him the evil eye for years now. Not that he cared; he hardly ever saw her. He just wasn't sure he wanted Shanna anywhere near her. Of course, he had no way of preventing her from seeing Lynn.

Shanna laughed. "She loves him."

"I rest my case."

She gave him a disparaging look. "You need a lot of work, *bwana*."

He raised his brows at her in his best mocking look, which she countered with a grin.

"You need to lighten up, Rand. I think we should give a party. Maybe a talent show. You and I could sing together—'You Are My Sunshine,' something like that."

He'd rather throw himself in front of a wounded buffalo. "I need a drink," he said with a groan and turned to go.

He heard her laughter behind him, clear, joyful. He caught himself smiling.

He caught himself smiling often.

A danger sign, no doubt.

CHAPTER NINE

"YOU'RE in a good mood today," Rosemary commented as she handed Rand the monthly financial statement. "Wouldn't have anything to do with Shanna coming back from Nairobi today?"

He gave her a cool look. "It's your sweet smile that makes my day."

She laughed. "You're such a charmer, Rand."

"Go pester your husband, I'm busy."

She left him, laughing, and he applied his attention to the report in front of him. That done, he grabbed his gun and drove off in a cloud of dust to the dam to check on the water level.

The house looked as it always had as he drove up at the end of the day. Still, he felt different about coming home these days.

The house smiles again, Kamau had said when Shanna had first moved in. Rand knew it was true, recognizing how his life had changed. Shanna filled the house, his life, with light and laughter and color. She'd only been gone three nights, but he had missed her. The house had seemed oddly empty without her, yet for years he'd lived in it all by himself. Had been perfectly content.

At least that's what he had told himself.

He thought about her finishing the manuscript and leaving to go back to Boston. How long would it be? Another three, four months? No doubt by then she would be happy to get back to city life.

Impatiently he got out of the car and slammed the door shut.

Her car was back, and he felt a little jolt seeing the green monster sitting by the side of the house, covered in red dust. She liked the damn thing, who'd have thought? She looked like she belonged in a Ferrari, with the wind blowing in her hair.

He heard her laughter as he entered the house. It came from the kitchen and he made his way there, the dogs following at his heels. She didn't notice him immediately and for a moment he stood there watching her.

She was barefoot, wearing a bright *kanga,* wrapped around her hips sarong-style, teamed with a skimpy white top. The Swahili proverb printed on the *kanga* read *Follow bees and you will get honey.* He wondered if she'd selected the cloth for its color and design, or for the proverb. Several strands of colorful native beads dangled from her neck, bouncing on her breasts as she moved. With Kamau's help she was unloading what looked like groceries from a couple of cardboard boxes. He glimpsed a bit of golden skin between her top and the *kanga* as she reached into the box.

He felt an instant hot urge to touch her, rip off that silly cloth, feel the satiny warmth of her naked skin against him. He closed his eyes for an instant, stunned by his own reaction, as if he were a teenager with galloping hormones. She turned and caught sight of him. Her eyes lit up and her face broke into a smile.

"Oh, hi! I didn't see you."

"I just got here. How are you?" As if he could not tell. She was perfectly fine, her eyes bright in her glowing face. Her hair was a windblown tangle, twisted loosely on top of her head.

"I had a great time! I went shopping with Lynn. We were all over Nairobi, the open market, Biashara Street. We had Ethiopian food at this funky little place and last night we were invited to a dinner party, out of the blue, and there were all these interesting people. A Hollywood producer, believe it or not, and this Washington reporter...."

He didn't hear everything she said, he just looked, at her bright eyes and happy face and dread began to creep into his heart like a slow poison.

She liked Nairobi. Of course she did. A big, vibrant colorful city with wonderful shops and excellent restaurants—why would she not?

"Look what I got," she was saying, waving at the stuff on the kitchen table. "Goat cheese, Camembert, Gorgonzola, walnuts, prosciutto, smoked trout. I am going to cook you a meal to die for. Oh, and look at this!" She picked up a box and held it out to him to see, like an offering. "Trada...an espresso machine!" She beamed up at him, and suddenly the smile washed right off her face. She stopped talking for a moment and stared at him, frowning. "What's wrong?"

"Nothing." He shook his head, rubbed his neck. "I'm happy you enjoyed yourself." Was he? What the hell was wrong with him?

"I did," she said, her tone low, a little hesitant. "It was fun running around town with Lynn." She bit her lip and he could see the puzzlement in her eyes. He turned away.

"I'm going to have a drink. Can I pour you one?"

There was only the slightest pause before she answered. "No, thank you. I'll go shower first."

He was just tired, Shanna thought, as she stood under the warm water, washing the red dust out of her hair. There was nothing wrong; she'd just imagined it.

She dried off with a big fluffy towel, and wrapped another one of her new *kangas* around her waist. *Mcheza kwao hutuzwa,* said the proverb—He who dances at home will be rewarded. Not bad advise at all, she thought, and grinned at her reflection in the mirror. The *kangas* had looked so gorgeous and colorful hanging and stacked up in the market, she hadn't been able to make a choice and just buy one. So she'd bought four, feeling wonderfully extravagant. Not that they were expensive, but still, four seemed rather a lot.

She opened a dresser drawer and fished out an emerald-green, lacy bra. A perfect match with the colors of the *kanga*. Too bad she'd have to cover it up with a top. But first her hair. It was dripping down her back. She rubbed at it with a towel and found her hair-dryer.

Rand came into the bedroom as she finished drying her hair, a glass of wine in his hand.

"Here," he said, handing it to her. "It's good to have you back." His eyes smiled into hers, full of warmth, of love.

There was nothing wrong. She'd just imagined it.

"And I'm happy to be back." She smiled back at him, wanting him to know the truth of it.

She came to her feet, liking the loose, comfortable feel of the thin cotton *kanga* against her legs. "What do you think?" She raised her arms, glass of wine still in her hand, and made a slow, seductive belly-dance twirl in front of him. "Don't you love the colors?"

He was sitting on the side of the bed and she stopped in front of him, pressing her legs lightly against his knees. She looked down into his face, taking a slow sip of her wine, teasing him with her eyes.

"Dance some more," he said, "so I can see better."

She made another seductive twirl with her hips, coming to rest again in front of him.

"Nice colors," he agreed.

Laughter bubbled up inside her. He was so understated, so cool, so…British.

"What's so funny?"

"You." She couldn't help the laughter and the next thing she knew he took the glass from her hand, put it down and with one swift movement twisted her around and tossed her down on the bed. He hovered above her.

"You're laughing at me," he said darkly.

"But not in a mean way," she said soothingly and bit her lip.

"Why? What did I say?"

"You said the colors were nice."

"And what's wrong with that? Wasn't that what you wanted to hear?"

"*Nice* is the best you can do? It's a nothing word. It has no spice, no shine. How about…oh…gorgeous, brilliant, exotic, sexy?"

"That's you," he said, "not that damn piece of cloth." And with that he reached out and yanked it right away from her hips.

"You're naked," he said.

"I'm sure you're scandalized."

He laughed softly and lowered his face against her naked belly. "I presume now that you've danced for me, you want your reward."

She felt the rasp of his rough chin, unshaven since morning, the warmth of his lips. She reached out and ran her fingers through his short, thick hair as desire rushed through her like a bushfire.

"That would be fair," she said, feeling suddenly breathless.

"You smell so good," he muttered. "And I am a filthy swine. I should go shower."

"I don't care," she whispered. He smelled of the bush, dust, sunshine, wood smoke. He smelled of him, the man she loved, and it felt like the most erotic sensation to have him close and breathe him in. She did not want to let him go.

Her body felt full, alive, like lush, ripe fruit ready to burst.

She felt the heat of his body warming her skin. "I'm so glad I'm back," she said on a sigh.

He raised his head, sliding up to look into her eyes. "Shanna," he said thickly.

"Don't go," she whispered, drawing his face down, kissing him. "Please, I want you."

I love you, she wanted to say, but she could not tell him the words. She could tell him with her body.

And she would tell him over and over, until he knew. Until he would no longer doubt her.

There were so many stories in this vast and wild land, so few secrets. Soon Shanna, too, was part of the local scene, picking up news at parties and other gatherings. Someone's child had been bitten by a snake and barely survived. Somebody's wife had been caught having an affair with a visiting scientist. Somebody was pregnant and the lover had flown off to another continent.

"What would you do if I found out that I was pregnant?" Shanna asked Rand impulsively. She saw him freeze, his hand tight around his whiskey glass.

"Are you?" he demanded.

"No," she said, "I'm not. Would be a statistical miracle, you know that."

"Yes, well it happens."

She gave him a searching look. "I wouldn't get pregnant intentionally to play some sort of manipulative game, Rand, if that's what you were thinking."

She wanted a baby of her own, but not like that. Never like that.

"Good." He picked up the bottle of Scotch and poured himself a generous measure.

"I'm just wondering what your reaction would be if it happened unintentionally. What would you do if I were pregnant?"

He scowled impatiently. "I have no intention of wasting time worrying about a hypothetical question." He took a deep drink from his glass and again she had the awful feeling that she was talking to a stranger.

"Would you abandon me, your child?"

His hand gripped the glass. "I told you—"

"It's not complicated, Rand. If I had your child, would you abandon it?"

He slammed the glass on the table, and whiskey spilled over the edge. "No," he ground out, his body rigid. "No, I would not abandon my own child!"

She was shaken by the vehemence of his reply and didn't know what to say. He glared at her. "I suppose I'd marry you," he said flatly.

"You're enthusiasm is flattering," she returned, equally coldly. "And your generosity is touching." She felt chilled to the bone.

"Well, what answer were you looking for?" he demanded.

Anger rose to her head. "It was a hypothetical question and I hope it never becomes a real one, because I'd never marry a man who wouldn't want me for myself."

He was about to say something in return, then apparently changed his mind. His eyes looked shadowed. He raked his hand down over his face, as if rubbing away thoughts, feelings. "What the hell was the point of this conversation?" he demanded.

She felt suddenly exhausted, emotionally more than physically. "I don't know," she said tonelessly. "Somewhere along the line I lost the point."

Why had she asked? Had she subconsciously wanted to test him? The thought appalled her. Sadness, heavy and solemn, settled over her. For a while neither one of them said anything. Rand finished his drink and put the glass down.

He was still standing by the bar. He moved toward her and sat down next to her on the sofa. He did not touch her.

"I know you want a baby of your own," he said, echoing her thoughts.

"That wasn't the question, Rand. I'd never get pregnant intentionally without the...father's consent."

He closed his eyes for a moment. "I'm not some unfeeling, selfish bastard, Shanna," he said wearily.

She swallowed. "I didn't say you were."

"Sometimes I feel you think I am."

"Sometimes I feel you want me to think you are."

"Why?" He looked surprised.

"Because you're afraid I'll like you too much." *Love you too much,* is what she wanted to say. "You don't want me too close. You want to keep me at a distance." It hurt to say the words, to express what she knew was true about him while she herself wanted nothing more than to open herself to him, let him know her thoughts, all the stirrings of her heart.

He did not answer her. She looked at his face.

"It's true, isn't it?" she said softly.

He closed his eyes, as if it was hard for him to look at her. "I want my life simple, uncomplicated."

"Am I making it not so?" she asked.

"No. But your question threw me off. I'm sorry, I was a bastard for reacting the way I did. I didn't mean to hurt you."

"It's all right."

But it wasn't all right. She felt a growing sense of doom. She wished she'd never asked the question.

Simple and uncomplicated is what he wanted. It's what *she* wanted. Why was that so hard?

He'd driven into Nyahururu for some business, decided to have a quick lunch and found himself ambushed by Antonia.

She'd spied him sitting on the sidewalk terrace, marched across the street and pulled up a chair. She wore slim-fitting black pants and a loose white shirt with the sleeves rolled up. An ornate silver Ethiopian cross hung around her neck and she looked ready for anything, as usual.

He watched her, vaguely amused by her, as he always was, this woman he had known all his life. Years ago she'd pursued him fervently and shamelessly, but had finally given up with good grace. She was intense, restless, demanding and he admired that husband of hers.

"So," she said, "fancy seeing you here all by your lonely self. What's new?"

"Not much."

She waved at a waiter, ordered chicken curry and a Tusker beer. "Do you mind?" she asked, as if she cared.

"Feel free," he said wryly.

She ignored his sardonic undertone. "So, how's Shanna? Haven't seen her for a while."

"She's doing well. Still working on her book. Learning to be quite a bush woman, too, shooting like a pro." Not that she wanted to kill anything living and moving, but he'd made her take a few practice shots at some francolins and she'd got one perfectly. Kamau had fixed the bird for dinner and she'd refused to eat it.

"Pretend it's quail, or just chicken," he'd told her. "You've eaten thousands of chickens in your life."

"But not this one," she'd said stubbornly. "It was alive and well this morning. And I saw it. And then I killed it. And I am not going to eat it."

Antonia's eyebrows shot up. "Shanna with a gun? Fabulous! I knew she had it in her." She grinned, and met his eyes. "So, are you going to marry the girl?"

He should have expected something like this, still the question took him by surprise. "No," he said brusquely, not inviting further comment.

"Why not?" Antonia was not easily deterred, he should have known. She looked at him sharply. "She'd be good for you," she added. "She's got spirit, pizzazz."

"She's going back to Boston."

"Did she say that?"

"It's understood." He took a swallow of his beer.

Antonia rolled her eyes, which he found irritating in the extreme. She leaned forward, arms on the table. "Understood by whom? You? Or her? Did you *ask* her?"

He looked straight into her eyes. "Antonia," he said calmly, "would you kindly mind your own damn business?"

"No," she said. "You're going to end up like your father, that mean-spirited cantankerous rotter. You'll end up all alone, in that big house, turning into a recluse with only your dogs for company."

"You paint a charming picture."

"And then one day you'll be tromping through the bush by yourself, break a leg or something and the lions will find you and the hyenas will finish you off if the vultures don't get to you first and no one will even miss you."

Her sense of drama made him smile. He patted her hand. "You will, Antonia, you will."

"For God's sake, Rand! You need a wife, kids! You need a life! What's keeping you?"

"I'm not interested."

"You *really* want to end up like your father?"

"You weren't fond of him, were you?" Not that that was much of a surprise. Few people had been.

"No." She glared at him. "He made your mother's life a living hell."

Anger rose to his head like a flood. "That's enough, Antonia."

"No! I loved your mother. Everybody did and you never wanted to hear that, did you? I don't know why you hate her so. She was a wonderful person and your father chased her away. Like you are doing. Like you did with Marina, like you're doing now with Shanna and—''

"Shut up," he said, and he heard the odd tone of his own voice, as if it wasn't his, but someone else's, coming from some deep, dark place, a place full of sadness and a young boy's grief. "You don't know what you're talking about."

"I know exactly what I am talking about! And it's about time someone enlightened you."

"Thank you, Dr. Freud," he said coldly. He threw some shilling notes on the table and came to his feet. He walked away, not even looking at her.

"How would you like to be swept away to a magical place?" Rand asked Shanna a week later.

"*This* is a magical place," she said, wondering what he was getting at.

It was almost dusk and they were sitting in the lookout, with a little picnic Kamau had prepared for them. An elephant noisily slurped water from the water hole, and monkeys messed around in the trees nearby.

"Another magical place. You've been working too hard and you need a change of scenery."

His confident pronouncements made her laugh. "I love working on the book. I don't need a rest, and the most gorgeous scenery in the world is right here. Haven't you noticed?" She took a leisurely sip of wine and couldn't imagine wanting to be anywhere else right now.

"There is different gorgeous scenery in other places, why not have a look? Just for a few days."

She frowned at him, surprised a little. "You want to go on a trip, really?"

"Yes. It will be my birthday gift to you."

She didn't know how he knew it was her birthday, but his generosity touched her. How much easier to have someone send a piece of jewelry from Nairobi, or some other kind of gift. Instead he was taking time off to be with her, away from his beloved ranch, away from his work.

"Really? You want to go away with me?"

He gave a lopsided smile. "Is that so strange?"

"Yes, no, I mean…I just thought you'd rather not leave here if you didn't have to."

"Let's see if I can handle it," he said dryly. "Three days."

"I'd love to go away for three days with you," she said solemnly, but her heart was doing a little waltz of happiness in her chest.

He smiled. "Good."

Besides, she thought, who could disagree with the fact that there were other places in the world with a beauty of their own? Not her, Shanna.

"Where?" she asked, feeling excitement begin to build.

"It's a surprise." It was all he was willing to divulge.

CHAPTER TEN

RAND had promised a surprise, and it certainly was.

"I can't believe this," Shanna said in awe as she took in the vista of white sand, palm trees and a blue-green ocean. Here she was, sitting on the deep, shady veranda of a beach house overlooking the Indian Ocean and a tall man in a long white robe and a small embroidered skull cap had just brought them a cool, coconut drink spiked with rum.

Only this morning she had awoken in the coolness of a Rift Valley dawn, and now she was here on the tropical Kenya coast, the sultry air full of the scents of the sea, of ripe mango, frangipani blossoms and coconut.

"I knew you'd like it," he said. "Happy birthday."

"Thank you." She felt a lump in her throat, felt silly to be so sentimental. "This is a wonderful present, Rand."

"You deserve it." His eyes glinted with humor as he looked at her. "Besides, a little fun and frivolity is good for the soul. Who said that? Confucius? Socrates?"

"Somebody brilliant like that," she said and he laughed.

The sun was setting, and on the horizon small fishing boats appeared, coming in with the catch of the day. Lobster was on the menu for tonight, Nazir, the cook, had told her, unless she preferred something else.

She did not.

"This is a gorgeous place," she said, leaning back lazily in her chair. The house was built of whitewashed coral stone, had a roof thatched with palm fronds and was open to the breezes from the ocean. The living room with its overstuffed cane furniture and antique African artwork exuded a welcoming, yet exotic ambience. Open-plan, it had arched doorways leading to various parts of the house, including a lovely interior courtyard with a profusion of flowering potted plants.

"You didn't tell me whose house this is," she said.

"It belongs to Antonia's parents. They sold their coffee farm a few years ago, and bought this place for their retirement. They're in Italy now, visiting family."

"Did Antonia tell you it was my birthday?"

"No." He gave her a smug little grin. "I saw it on your driver's license when you showed me your stunning mug shot."

"Oh, yes." She laughed. The picture looked like it belonged on a Wanted poster—her person wanted for some dire crime with an award worth a small fortune.

He had noticed her birthdate and had remembered it. It warmed her sentimental little heart.

They slept that night in a big bed under white mosquito netting, to the sound of the waves breaking on the coral reef.

Next morning they explored the small town while friendly merchants tried to persuade them to buy some of their wares—fruit, baskets, soapstone, wood carvings.

"*Bwana!* Your wife, she likes this! I will give you a good price!"

She'd made the mistake of picking up a soapstone bowl to look at it better.

"*Bwana,* you must buy it for her! A man must not disappoint his wife!"

She put the bowl down and shook her head, laughing. "No, no, thank you."

So Rand bought it for her anyway.

They moved on through the ancient, narrow streets with their whitewashed houses and Arab architecture, the air rich with the scent of spices and sandalwood oil.

The merchant had thought she was Rand's wife. Well, not so strange, was it?

"Why have you never married?" she asked impulsively, moving aside as a herd of goats squeezed her for space.

Maybe she should not have asked, but it had come out automatically. What was wrong with asking, anyway? She was sleeping in his bed, living in his house. She was tired of worrying about what she could ask and what was taboo.

He shrugged. "I never wanted to."

Well, that answer was clear.

"Don't you want kids? Teach them to hunt and fish and swim."

"I don't see myself as having kids, no. How's this?" He indicated a little rooftop restaurant, overlooking the town.

"Looks interesting." *I wish you would talk to me.*

"You're ready for some traditional Swahili food?"

I'm ready for anything. Especially a little more insight into what makes you tick, the truth about why you've never married.

"Absolutely," she said. "Lots of coconut and spices?"

"Right."

In ages past, Arab traders had brought the spices, as well as their genes, religion and architecture, and the coastal area of Kenya was like a different country.

Following the arrow on a handmade wooden sign, they moved up a narrow stone staircase. The restaurant was small but airy, festooned with an abundance of flowering vines and plants. Blue and white tablecloths cheerily draped over the small tables, of which there were five.

"Looks like somebody set up shop on the roof of his house," she said, sitting down at one of the tables.

The proprietor, dressed in white, sporting the ubiquitous little embroidered cap, greeted them with a smile and after a few pleasantries told them what was on offer that day, lamb in a spicy coconut sauce, a dish his wife had cooked herself and which was famous in the town.

"We are lucky people," Shanna said and smiled at the man, who departed to take care of their order.

The cold bottle of water they'd ordered arrived and Shanna took a grateful drink, enjoying the view over the rooftops, with the ocean glittering in the distance. Her mind was still working on the unfinished discussion, wouldn't leave it alone.

Rand had never wanted to be married, or so he said. They'd never talked about it before, personal discussions always avoided by him.

"I want to talk to you," she said, feeling suddenly reckless.

Rand leaned back in his chair and stretched out his legs. "Fire away."

"I have questions."

"You always have questions."

"True. But maybe you don't want to hear these questions."

"Then don't ask them." He took a drink from his water and gazed out over the rooftops.

"I *want* to ask them, Rand. And I want you to answer them and I don't want you to get angry or be evasive or anything like that."

"You're being very demanding, *memsab,*" he said lightly.

Clearly she wasn't getting very far with this discussion. She'd better just dive right in. "I asked you why you've never married and you said you never wanted to. Why?"

"Sounds like you're planning an interview."

This did not sound promising. Oh, never mind, she thought irritably, whatever works.

"Right. It's for another article I'm writing," she lied. "It's called *The Secret Love Life of a White Hunter.*" She was amazed she managed to keep a straight face.

"Fascinating," he said, not fooled for a moment.

From the minaret of the small mosque nearby, the muezzin began his chanting, calling the faithful to prayer. It lent a rather exotic flavor to the surroundings.

"Why didn't you ever want to be married, Rand?"

"It never worked out that way."

"Why? Can't you be a little more...specific?"

"No," he said, his tone light.

"Why did you ask me to move in with you?"

"Because you promised me free access to your body."

Her mouth dropped open. "I did no such thing," she said, outraged.

He laughed out loud. "I so love to shock you."

The owner of the restaurant brought them their food. Delicious aromas wafted forth from the plates.

"If this tastes as good as it smells, perhaps you should ask for the recipe," said Rand, clearly looking for a change of subject. *"Bon appétit."*

"I wasn't finished, you know," she said, picking up her fork and knife. "So if I understand it correctly, you invited me for the sex."

"Right." He forked in a bite of lamb.

"And before me there was Marina."

His eyes narrowed. "Yes."

He had never spoken of Marina to her and Shanna had never mentioned her in all the time she'd lived on the ranch.

"And before her?"

"Suzy."

"And before Suzy?"

"Wendy."

"And before her?"

"Mindy."

"Suzy, Wendy, Mindy. Have I got it right?"

"Yes."

"And they all lived with you?"

"Right."

"You're lying through your teeth."

"I thought I'd try it out and see how it felt."

She rolled her eyes at him. "Tell me something that's true."

"You have very sexy feet. I'm especially enamored of that blue nail polish."

It was, to say the least, a very unfruitful discussion. But at least, he wasn't angry, which she didn't want. Spoiling this meal, even the rest of the day would be sad; she hadn't been very bright starting this conversation at this time at all.

Still, she was tired of his evasions, his clamming up. She was really, really tired of it. Sooner rather than later she was going to deal with it.

But now was not the time. Determinedly she pushed all thoughts of confrontation out of her mind and concentrated on the food in front of her.

This was the time for romance and dreams and illusion. She was here with Rand in this fun little rooftop restaurant eating delicious food, the flavors hinting of history and far-away places.

Later they went to the beach and lay in the shade of a coconut palm and read, and dozed, and talked, taking swims intermittently to cool off.

"I feel positively decadent lying here doing absolutely nothing of any redeeming social value," she said with a languorous sigh.

"I like you decadent," he said.

She sighed again. "You are so good for me, Mr. Rand Caldwell."

Rand listened to Shanna talking about her parents that night, over another lobster dinner, which she had asked for. Her opinion was that one could never eat enough lobster, especially not when it was cheap and fresh off the fishing boats. He wasn't going to argue with her.

He watched her face in the flickering candlelight, listened to her voice as she told of her mother, her father, her voice rich and sweet with emotion. He could listen to that voice all night.

She told him that along with her grief and denial about their death, she had been furious with them for leaving her behind, alone.

"I dreamed about wanting to *sue* them," she said, putting her fork and knife down. "Nights in a row. Can you *believe* that?"

He couldn't help but smile at the amazed disapproval in her voice, and somewhere in a hidden part of him he was aware of a sense of recognition. "Certainly, I can. You're not the furniture-smashing type."

"No, but I would have understood it better. I mean, dragging my parents into court wasn't exactly a physical possibility, but how could I *want* to do that? To the people I loved most in the world!"

He understood it perfectly. He wished he didn't. He remembered well the anger and the betrayal he had felt when his mother had left. The terrible things he had thought.

"Because you wanted them back, and you were very angry, obviously."

She sighed. "Yes, at everything and everybody—my parents, God, the universe. I thought something was really wrong with me and then I talked to the mother of one of my college friends who happens to be a family counselor and she said it was normal." She grinned suddenly. "Scary, huh?"

"Lots of strange things are normal."

She laughed. "May we find comfort in that." She lifted her wineglass. "Let's toast to a strange and wonderful world."

He had no problem with that.

Two days later, lying in his own bed at the ranch, her words came back to him—*a strange and wonderful world.*

He glanced at the tangle of blond hair on the pillow next to his. That's how she looked at the world, at life. Strange and wonderful. It often surprised him how much pleasure she found in even the most simple things. A strange insect, a beautiful bird, a nice meal, a colorful *kanga* with some funny proverb. *Kindness does not go rotten. He who sows disorderly fashion will eat likewise.* Her laughter came easily, and he loved the sound of it.

And one day he would lose her, and his world would no longer be strange and wonderful.

Shanna was dancing barefoot in the grass, her *kanga* swaying around her legs. She was in an exuberant mood for no other reason than it felt wonderful to be alive and the man she loved was striding toward her across the lawn. He was the most wonderfully sexy man with his blue, blue eyes, and his tall body moving with such easy confidence. She could look at him forever.

Having reached her he put his hands in his pockets and watched her with amusement, so she went right on dancing, twirling around and waving her hips and arms to a rhythm of her own.

"Have I told you lately?" she asked airily.

"Told me what?"

That I love you, the old song went in her head.

"That I love this gorgeous place," she said instead. "That I love waking up next to you every morning. That I love making love with you. That I love our walks in the bush. That I love listening to your voice." She dropped herself into the grass, a little breathless, and gazed up at the wide, blue sky.

"That I can't imagine ever wanting to leave."

Leaning back on her arms, she kept looking up into the

vast blueness, hearing the birds twittering in the fever tree nearby.

Hearing the pounding of her own heart.

How many ways could she tell him she loved him without saying the words? Words she knew instinctively he did not want to hear.

He sat down next to her, forearms leaning on his knees. She glanced at him sideways, but his face was in shadow.

"You've been bewitched," he said lightly. "Like everybody who comes to this country. You're under its spell."

"I'm not everybody." Disappointment was bitter in her mouth.

"I'm sorry, that's not how I meant it."

It was exactly how he meant it. She was appalled at the tears burning behind her eyes. "You think my feelings are not real."

"I think they're real, just—"

"You think it's just a passing fancy. It's been *months,* Rand." Months of hoping he would want to see the truth of her feelings, want to tell her his own.

"I don't want you to get hurt, in the end," he said roughly.

She turned over and sat on her knees in front of him, looking right into his face, the face she loved with all her heart. "Why would I get hurt?"

"By becoming too attached, by thinking that this life is what you want."

"Would it be so bad if I did?"

He rubbed his face. "It's just not going to last. It's not going to work, not in the end. It would be better to be realistic about it, to enjoy what we have until you have to leave."

I don't have to leave, she wanted to say, but the words stuck in her throat.

He brushed his hand over her cheek. "Let's keep it simple," he said. "All right?"

She sat back and pulled her knees to her chin, looking away from him toward the ancient hills, smoky blue in the distance.

"Is that what happened with Marina?" she asked softly. "Did it get too complicated?"

When he didn't immediately answer, she turned to look at him. His expression was closed and withdrawn. He didn't want to discuss Marina.

"What happened with Marina?" she insisted.

"She wasn't happy here," he said flatly.

She said she'd had enough of living with someone who kept her at an emotional distance all the time. Lynn's words sprang into her consciousness.

"Why not?"

His jaw grew steely. "Not many women can tolerate this kind of isolated life for very long. And I am not discussing Marina with you, Shanna."

"Rosemary is happy living here," she went on, not wanting to be put off. "And Antonia certainly doesn't have any trouble with it, and she lives even farther up north. She has a life of her own, makes documentaries, flies her own plane, goes to Nairobi when she feels like it. "

He gave an impatient shrug. "They both grew up here. They know this place. They belong here."

So that's what it was.

His mother was American. Marina was Australian. And here she was also a foreigner.

"So it's a *wazungu* thing? It's foreigners who can't stand the life here for the long haul?"

"It's not an insult," he said wearily. "It's reality."

"It's *prejudice.* I'd have appreciated it if you could see me as an individual, and not an anonymous, statistical member of some foreign tribe."

For some reason this made him smile a little. "You are very much *not* an anonymous, statistical member of some foreign tribe to me, Shanna."

She took a deep breath. "Then prove it. Don't judge me by what other women did."

She thought of his mother, seeing in her mind the photo at Antonia's house. For someone who didn't like the lifestyle in the bush, she certainly seemed to have adapted well.

Rand looked at her, his eyes dark and unreadable. "Shanna, I don't want you to get the wrong idea."

She swallowed. "And what is that?"

"I don't want you to think there's a future here. Marriage, children, whatever you've been thinking."

She felt suddenly icy-cold. She struggled to her feet, stared down at him still sitting in the grass. "Well, I'm glad we've got that cleared up."

He didn't like her looking down at him, she could tell. He stood up, raked his hand through his hair.

"Shanna, you're going back to Boston, sooner or later."

"What makes you so sure? Is there a law that says so? Is it written on stone tablets?" Anger and frustration fought for dominance.

"Don't be so damned naive, Shanna! For God's sake, be realistic!"

She felt herself begin to tremble. She wanted to say something terrible, shout at him, but nothing came out of her throat. Hugging herself hard she tried to calm herself, to stop the trembling.

She felt sick. She had never felt for a man what she was feeling for Rand. She could not explain it—it was deep and true and honest. It came from the very depth of her heart and had nothing to do with reason or logic.

If she allowed reason and logic to take part, she would pack up and go now. All the signs were wrong. All the omens spelled heartbreak and disaster. Everybody had warned her.

She would never get over it. Never.

I'm not leaving, she said to herself. *He can't make me.*

"Shanna?"

His voice seemed to come from far away.

"Shanna, don't look like this, please!" His arms came around her, held her against him and she did not resist.

"Damn it, I'm sorry," he said in a strangled voice. "I don't mean to hurt you. I just—"

He just wanted to be realistic. And to him that meant there would come an end to their relationship. In the end she would leave. So he thought. So he knew. To him it was a given. His mother had left. Marina had left.

And of course, she would leave.

She felt a deep, aching pain—for him, for herself.

And then she felt a surge of new strength, of new hope.

She would prove him wrong. She wasn't leaving, like the others.

Her face against his shoulder, she made herself calm down, taking in a few deep, slow breaths. This was where she wanted to be, right here, in his arms.

She turned her face, put her lips against his warm neck. "I'm not leaving," she whispered.

So she played the game and made it simple. No mentioning of the future, no mentioning of the past, at least not his.

There was just the present.

And the present was wonderful—full of love and laughter and the adventure of living in paradise.

But how long, she asked herself, could a person live in a bubble, no matter how lovely?

"Mail for you," Rand said and handed Shanna an envelope that had arrived with the business mail Rosemary had collected from the post office that morning.

He watched her face, a little pale and nervous suddenly as she read the return address. Her hand trembled as she ripped the envelope open, sitting down at the table set for lunch. Photos slid out into her hand. She spread them out on the table to the side of her plate.

Baby photos. He saw a happy, smiling child, playing, laughing. Shanna looked at them silently, her face soft, her mouth trembling.

"He's so big now," she said quietly.

He had no idea what to say to this, but he felt his gut twist at the look of longing in her eyes. But she wasn't crying, thank God for that.

"Babies change so much so fast," she said pensively. She gathered the photos and slipped them back in the envelope. "I'll just put these away," she said, her voice calm. Too calm.

All afternoon he had a rotten feeling crawling through him, and he couldn't quite figure out what it was. Until he saw one of the village women walking by on the road with a baby tied on her back.

The feeling was guilt.

He thought if Shanna, of the longing in her eyes. Longing for a child that was not hers, she could never have. She was a woman and she wanted children. What was wrong with that?

Nothing, except that he had told her he wasn't going to take part in a scenario of that sort. Not to expect from him anything permanent.

In the meantime, he was sleeping with her. What a prince of a fellow he was.

And she is sleeping with you, came the instant, defensive thought. She was here out of her own free will. She could leave anytime she wanted to.

But she didn't want to.

Because she loved him.

Well, he'd heard that before and it hadn't done him a lot of good, in the end. Love. It was nothing but a temporary illusion.

The rotten feeling didn't go away.

It filled the office, his car, his head. It had a smell, a taste, a color. It engulfed him.

Do you really want to end up like your father? Antonia's voice was clear in his mind. *You'll end up all alone, in that big house, turning into a recluse with only your dogs for company.*

He cursed under his breath. Antonia and her melodrama— why did he spend any energy contemplating her ridiculous scenarios?

Shanna looked at Sammy's pictures for the umpteenth time, reread the note from a social worker she did not know, telling her Sam was doing beautifully in his new home. Along with the pain of seeing the pictures had come another feeling—the relief to feel reassured once again that Sammy was loved and cared for, that he was a happy baby giving his adoptive parents much joy. He had a father and a mother, and he had settled in well with them. Just knowing it and seeing the pictures made her feel better.

So why was she sitting here with the tears running down her cheeks?

It was time to let Sammy go, really go. She needed to look to her own future now.

And she knew what she wanted. She wanted Rand. She wanted marriage and not some loose-end affair. She wanted babies of her own. Maybe sitting back and waiting for Rand to change his ideas was futile.

She had to think of something.

Walking helped, so she walked, and ended up in the workers' village and at Rosemary's house.

Rosemary was taking a doorknob apart, trying to figure out why it wasn't working properly.

Shanna laughed. "One day I'm going to find you on top of the roof fixing a leak."

"I've done that," said Rosemary, deadpan, then grinned. "I'm glad you're here. I've really got to talk to somebody."

"Me, too," said Shanna. "You first."

They sat on the veranda with a glass of cold pineapple juice and Rosemary could barely contain herself.

"I'm pregnant," she said, her face all aglow with the excitement of it.

"Oh, Rosemary, that's wonderful! I'm so happy for you!"

"I can't believe it. We've tried for a year and I was getting ready to do something drastic, and bingo, here I am, in the family way."

"And you didn't have to take anything apart and fix it," Shanna said, unable to resist. "When did you know?"

So they talked about that for a few minutes until Rosemary wanted to hear what Shanna had on her mind.

"I'm ready to do something drastic about Rand."

"Mmm," said Rosemary. "I could try taking his head apart and tinkering with his brain for you, see if we can put some sense into it."

Shanna laughed. "Thank you. You're very generous."

"Don't mention it."

"Alternatively, I could try shock therapy."

Rosemary gave her a thoughtful look. "Like telling him you're leaving if he doesn't change his ways?"

"Like asking him to marry me."

CHAPTER ELEVEN

ONE night, a week later, Rand came home and found the dining room soft and dreamy with candlelight. Sensuous music played in the background, mesmerizing. An exotic red tablecloth, woven through with an elaborate pattern in gold thread draped over the table. He had never seen it before. A profusion of flowers spilled from a copper bowl. A bottle of champagne waited in an ice bucket.

And Shanna, in a stunning brandy-colored dress, smiled at him, her green eyes glittering like emeralds in the soft light.

"Are we expecting dinner guests?" he inquired, knowing the answer as soon as he realized only two plates graced the table.

She gave him a feathery little kiss. "No. It's just us."

He held out a chair for her. "Well, then, what is this in honor of?"

"The book. It's finished. I sent it off this morning." She sat down and smiled up at him.

"I didn't realize…" Confusion muddled his brain. "I hadn't expected you to be finished so soon." She hadn't mentioned it either, given no indication that she was coming close to the end.

"It went really fast, in the end. I never really knew how long it would take me, except that my contract gave me a year, so more than that I didn't have."

Seven months it had taken her. Seven months she had lived here with him. He did not want to think about what was going to happen now. Right now he needed to be calm.

"Congratulations," he said, smiling at her. "Shall I open the champagne?"

"Please."

He opened the bottle, filled their two glasses and handed her one.

"Wish me luck," she said, raising her glass.

"All the luck in the world," he said, meaning it.

Now she was going to pack her things and go back to Boston. He didn't want to think about that right now.

Kamau came in with the soup. It was a lovely pale spring green.

"It's cold," she said. "I hope you like it. It's an experiment."

"I'm not worried in the least. Your experiments have come out splendidly, always."

"Thank you," she said solemnly, and picked up her spoon.

He began to eat, and indeed, it was delicious—fruity, minty with the tang of lime. He smiled at her across the table. In the candlelight her face was soft and sweet. He loved her face.

He didn't want to think about that either.

"So, what's going to happen next with the book?"

"Oh, editing, revisions. I'll probably go to New York and meet with my editor once or twice. And after that, who knows. They want to include photographs, and I'll sort through my father's collection and see if there's anything suitable. It's all going to take time. The book won't be on the shelves for a while yet."

She looked beautiful and happy and excited. He finished his wine and poured another glass. Champagne with soup. Well, why not.

"Are you glad it's finished now?"

"In a way. But I'm a little sad, too. I mean, it was a

wonderful project, and I so enjoyed doing it and now it's over.'' She sighed regretfully.

''Yes.''

And his life with her was over, too, but that's just how it was meant to be. It would have been better if he'd had a little warning though, so he could get used to the idea. He realized he'd finished his soup and hadn't tasted a thing after the first few spoonfuls.

She chatted on about the book, but he found it hard to concentrate. He kept looking at her face, the way it moved, her mouth, the candlelight reflected in her eyes.

Kamau came in to take away the soup plates and bring in the main course.

He wished the dinner was over. Wished the damned erotic music stopped filling the air with promise. He did not want to sit here and make polite conversation. What the hell was going on with her?

Nothing was going on with her. She was happy. She'd finished her project. She was going back to Boston. He took his wine and gulped it down. He didn't like champagne, never had.

''I think we need something else with this,'' he said, looking at the platter of artistically presented food on the table. He had no idea what it was, but it looked like meat was part of the composition. A wonderful seductive aroma reached his nose. ''What is it?''

''It's a Moroccan *tagine*,'' she said. ''Lamb with saffron and almonds and apricots and spices. There's a bottle of red wine behind you, on the sideboard.''

Kamau should have opened it and poured it, he thought irritably, and stood up to take care of it.

He poured the wine and sat down again. ''And what are your plans now that the book is finished?'' he asked casually.

''Oh,'' she said, ''seeing my advanced age, I think I'm

going to find myself a husband and have some children. Write another book, take up photography, live happily ever after, that sort of thing.''

''Sounds like a plan,'' he said, and finished his glass.

''Oh, and I want to learn how to fly an airplane.''

''I see. You're very ambitious, aren't you?''

''Absolutely.'' She raised her glass at him. ''I am ambitious, very ambitious.''

He saw the odd glitter in her eyes, felt his stomach tighten in apprehension. Something was going on with her. She drank her wine, carefully sipping. She put the glass down, and pushed her plate away. She had hardly eaten anything.

''There's something I want to tell you.'' Her voice sounded nervous, suddenly.

He put his knife and fork down and looked at her. Her eyes were huge. She ran her tongue over her lips.

''I love you, Rand.''

''I know.'' His voice was flat, coming from far away. He felt icy cold.

''Please, let's get married,'' she said.

He heard the words, knew she had spoken them, didn't want to take them in, acknowledge them. He shook his head, fighting panic.

And then the panic changed into anger.

Why the hell was she asking? She knew the answer. He had been clear, quite clear about his intentions from the very beginning. He could feel the anger empower him, flood him with heat and strength. She was not being fair, she...

She shoved her chair back and stood up. ''I just thought I'd ask,'' she said, her voice like that of a stranger—cool, calm, businesslike.

She moved to the door, and he watched her, seeing her as if in slow motion. She put her hand on the door, opened it. She stopped, turned to look at him.

''By the way, I'm driving to Nairobi tomorrow. I'll be at

Lynn's for a couple of days. She's throwing an impromptu party for me, to celebrate."

The door closed behind her.

He stayed in his chair, unable to move.

Kamau came in to take the dishes away, returning from the kitchen with the dessert, a chocolate mousse confection in the shape of a heart, with raspberries and cream.

He closed his eyes. "Take it away. We won't have it now."

"Ndiyo, bwana."

The room was quiet. The music had stopped. From outside came the sound of the wind in the trees. Then the scream of a jackal. He stared at the scarlet tablecloth, ran his finger over the thick gold threads woven into the red silk and suddenly recognition dawned.

It wasn't really a tablecloth at all. It was an Indian wedding sari.

"You look like hell," Rosemary said to him the next morning. "What's wrong?"

He just glared at her in answer and she raised her hands in apology.

"Sorry I asked."

He marched into his office and slammed the door. He couldn't face the paperwork and the room closed in on him. He'd hardly slept, lying next to an equally awake Shanna. He'd thought she might have gone to the guest room to sleep, but she hadn't. He'd felt like the worst bastard in the world, and here she was, still in bed next to him. He couldn't figure her out.

Rosemary came in with a cup of coffee. She never brought him coffee.

"I thought you might want this."

"Thank you," he said, trying to sound dismissive.

"I know her book is finished. Are you going to let her leave?"

"Mind your own business, Rosemary, or you're fired."

She laughed. "Ha, you need me too much."

Unfortunately this was true.

He pretended to read the file in front of him.

She leaned her skinny hip against his desk and crossed her arms. "I have a radical idea," she said casually. "Marry her."

A sure road to hell.

"I don't remember asking for your suggestions. Now get out of here."

She let out a long-suffering sigh. "You are a lost cause, *bwana*." She straightened away from the desk and strolled to the door. Then, as if something occurred to her, she turned to face him.

"By the way, I heard Marina got married last month."

"Thank you for informing me," he said coldly.

"She married an Aussie cattle rancher. Big spread way out in the Outback."

"And you're telling me this why?"

"Oh, I thought it might be of interest in case you have any illusions about why she left you." She paused, holding his gaze with her steady brown one. "I don't think it was because she didn't like the isolated lifestyle on the ranch." She opened the door and waltzed out.

He couldn't stand being in this office for another minute. He jammed his hat on his head and grabbed his rifle. He'd go check on the herds, check on the new bore holes, check on the fencing. Anything.

Rosemary looked meaningfully at the gun as he marched past her desk.

"Remember," she said darkly, "there are laws in this country."

*   *   *

He had arrived where he didn't want to be. Marrying her would only lead to disaster and he had no intention of fooling himself by denying it, by hoping it would not be so, thinking Shanna was different.

If she didn't believe him, he would simply have to show her. It was better for all concerned if she would leave sooner rather than later. It made no sense postponing the inevitable. It would only get more difficult, more painful—he knew from bitter experience.

He tried not to think of what his life would be like once she was gone.

Colorless. Dry as the desert.

In the distance a herd of elephants plodded across the land, searching for water.

Shanna did her best to enjoy the party Lynn had organized for her, but as she talked and laughed with the other guests, her mind kept going back to her botched dinner with the ridiculous red-and-gold tablecloth and the heart-shaped dessert.

What an idiot she had been.

Had she thought she could make Rand want to marry her if she lit some candles, poured some champagne and fed him a sensuous Moroccan dinner?

No, not really. Still, asking him to marry her had seemed a rather momentous occasion worthy of a bit of pomp and circumstance.

Which she had produced.

How could she have been so stupid?

"So, I hear you are leaving."

Shanna turned to look at the woman who'd materialized at her side. "Really?" she said coolly.

She'd met the woman once before and had felt an instinctive dislike. She couldn't imagine Lynn had invited her.

She'd probably trailed along with someone else. What was her name? Something like Lulu or Lola.

"Your book is finished, I understand," said Lulu/Lola. You must be happy." Her tone was not full of warm fuzzy sentiment. The woman had the nasty look and all the charm of a vulture.

Shanna stared at her. "Yes, I am happy." About the book being finished, at any rate.

The woman took a sip from her drink, a lurid green concoction. "When are you going back to the States?" she inquired.

"I am not," Shanna said coolly.

"Really now? You don't harbor any fantasies about hanging on to our friend Rand, do you?"

Shanna couldn't believe the woman's audacity. Was she waiting for her departure so she could move in for the kill and have Rand for herself? Shanna took a fortifying sip of wine. Well, she knew how to handle aggressive types like her.

She offered a careless shrug. "Oh," she said casually, "why not? He's drop-dead gorgeous, I like living at his ranch and I've made lots of friends. Not a bad life. Who wants to go back to Boston, right?" She could play shallow with the best of them.

The woman's predatory eyes narrowed as she evaluated Shanna's words.

"You know why he asked you to stay, don't you?" she said nastily.

"Sure." Shanna said, taking a leisurely sip of her drink. "I'm a great cook."

Lulu/Lola stared at her, her mouth dropping. Shanna almost laughed.

"You don't think that's it?"

"He asked you to stay because you were a safe bet," Lady Charm said venomously.

"A safe bet?" Shanna asked before she could help herself. Why was she asking? Why did she even listen to this hateful woman who'd had too much to drink?

"You were safe because you'd leave again," she said patiently, as if explaining something to a dim-witted child. "You'd finish your book and go back home. Very convenient for him. No commitment required or expected."

Shanna widened her eyes and feigned a look of surprise. "Oh, so you think he's not serious about me?" She might as well play the idiot; she seemed to do pretty well in that role lately.

"Damn right, darling." Miss Vulture tossed back the rest of whatever bilious potion she had in her glass. "He's never been serious about any woman, and don't flatter yourself thinking you're the exception."

"Does that please you?" Shanna felt a sudden cold rage at this loathsome woman, feeling in the depth of her the bitter truth of her words.

The woman stared at her for a moment, taken aback by her question.

"Why should that please me?" she snapped.

"Because you seem to take cruel pleasure in enlightening me. I don't get the impression you have a very generous spirit. I'd work on it if I were you."

And then, before she lost it all together, she turned away and walked down the stone steps into the dark, moonlit garden. Her legs were shaking. She hugged herself, fighting a sudden onslaught of despair.

Everybody knew. Everybody had warned her, kindly in most cases. She'd thought she could prove them wrong. Thought she could...would...

Her love was not enough and she had no idea what else to do. How could she love him more? Better? What was the magic she needed to make him trust her enough to open himself up to her?

She walked farther into the shadowy garden, letting the tears come, without fighting. Defeat was such a hopeless feeling.

"Shanna?" Out of the dark came Lynn's voice, urgent. "What did that witch say to you? I saw her talking to you, I saw her face."

Shanna shrugged, wiped her eyes with the back of her hand. She had no tissues with her.

"Are you crying? What did she say to you?"

Shanna swallowed miserably. "She said what everybody else has said. The same old thing."

"I thought things are working out between you and Rand." Lynn's voice sounded low and defeated.

"It only looks that way. Everybody is right, and I was wrong and I am finally beginning to admit it to myself, that's all."

"Oh, Shanna," Lynn said helplessly. "Come here." She put her arms around her and hugged her.

"I feel so stupid," Shanna said thickly. "I walked into this with my eyes wide open and still I was blind as a bat."

"Love will do that to you." Lynn turned her around and nudged her into the direction of the house. "Come on, let's go in and get smashed."

Shanna gave a choked little laugh. She couldn't help it. "That's a terrible idea."

"I know, but it was worth a shot to make you laugh."

With a prayer to the gods of love and good fortune, Shanna set off for the ranch the next day. It was a long drive back and it gave her plenty of time to think. Plenty of time to energize her sad soul, let the dry wind blow away her feelings of defeat. By the time she'd rolled passed Nyahururu she'd managed to talk herself into a more hopeful frame of mind.

She loved the drive back to the ranch, the open spaces, the hills in the distance, the endless sky.

Impala leaped away across the fields, swift and skittish. Giraffe calmly fed on acacia trees. The mud hut villages smelled of wood smoke and dust and goats—familiar and somehow comforting. Smiling children waved at her by the side of the road.

"Jambo! Jambo!" they shouted, their eyes full of curiosity and dreams.

"Jambo!" she returned, sticking her arm out the window and waving back, returning the smile.

A family of warthogs trotted off into the bushes as she drove by, their scrawny tails straight up in the air like hairy antennae. It was such a silly sight, she laughed.

She could still laugh.

And she hadn't given up.

Rand watched Shanna as she joked with Kamau about the mystery foods she had foraged from the supermarkets in Nairobi, some of which were now on the dining room table before him. Her Swahili was really good, he noticed not for the first time.

She'd returned in a relentlessly cheerful mood, as if nothing was wrong. Coming home at dusk, he'd found her on the veranda sipping a drink and reading a fashion magazine, looking fresh as an English spring morning in a fluttery yellow dress.

He looked at her now, across the table as she laughed with Kamau as he served up dinner, and for a terrifying moment he felt his resolve slipping.

He did not want her to leave. He wanted her.

He wanted to slip that skimpy yellow thing right off her body and have his way with her right there in the dining room, make love to her so all his doubts and fears would dissolve and disappear forever.

Wanted some fairy to wave a magic wand and make everything all right.

Instead, he made a minimum of polite conversation with her while they ate, after which he went back to his study and stayed there until well after midnight.

She was asleep when he entered the bedroom. The light was still on, the book she'd been reading open in the middle of the bed. She'd been waiting for him. Her hair gleamed in the light, her face looked soft in sleep. His heart churned painfully and he forced away the feeling, steeling himself.

He got ready for bed, turned off the light, lay on his back and stared at the dark ceiling, trying not to think of her lying next to him, trying not to hear her breathing.

"I'm not playing your game, Rand." Shanna faced him squarely. She could not stand it anymore. For days now he had been alien and distant, hardly speaking to her, lying in bed next to her, not touching her. The tension was terrible and the temptation to move back to the guest room ever present. But that would be giving in, the beginning of the end.

I'm not giving up, she thought, and felt her jaws clench in sympathy with her resolve.

"And what game is that?" he asked, not even looking up from his newspaper.

"You're pushing me away on purpose, but it's not going to work. I'm not leaving. Not on my own account, not voluntarily."

His manners got the better of him apparently, because he put his paper down and looked at her. Still, he did not speak, just waiting for her to go on.

So she did.

"You can get rid of me easily enough if that's what you want, Rand. You could physically throw me out. Pack me in your plane and fly me back to Nairobi. That would work, of course. But that's not how you want it to work, is it?''

''I have no idea what you're trying to say. I haven't asked you to leave.''

''No. The way you want it is for me to leave of my own accord so that your crazy theories are proven right once more. Well, you're wrong. You're wrong about me. I'm not Marina, and I'm not your mother and—''

''Leave my mother out of this!'' He threw the paper on the floor next to his chair as if the thing had offended him.

''No, I'm not! Your mother is the reason you treat me the way you do! You think because she didn't stay, no one else will either.''

He was pale under his tan. He came to his feet, pushed his hands into his pockets, looking down at her with unreadable eyes, saying nothing.

She took a deep breath. ''I'm like her, am I not?'' she said softly. ''I'm the happy, cheerful type, just like her. I like having fun and laughing and dancing. Just like her. And I have green eyes, just like her.'' She kept looking straight into his eyes as she spoke, seeing nothing but darkness.

''Well, let me tell you, Rand,'' she went on. ''Maybe I'm like her in some respects, I don't know. I've never met her. I'm not going to pass judgment on her character when all I know is hearsay and gossip.''

''How very commendable,'' he said derisively. ''Well, I did know her.''

''And you think I'm like her and you're judging me by your opinion of her. You decided I'd be good for a while, whatever time I was going to be here. You'd enjoy my company and you'd enjoy me in bed. And that's as far as it would go, isn't that right?''

His jaw went rigid. He moved away from her, picked up the newspaper from the floor and tossed it on the sofa. ''I made no promises.''

''No, you didn't. You want your life easy and uncomplicated. That's what you say, that's what you tell yourself.
But that's not the truth, is it? The real truth is that you're
scared. You, the big tough hunter who faces lions and rhinos
without blinking an eye. You are afraid of your own feelings, terrified you'll be hurt again. So you close yourself off
emotionally and won't let anybody in. Not Marina, not me.''

''You've got it all worked out, haven't you? Quite the
little psychoanalyst you are.''

She ignored his mockery. She was on a roll and she
wasn't going to let him stop her now. Getting up from her
chair, she moved right in front of him and looked up at his
cool, closed face. ''You chased her away,'' she said. ''You
pushed her away, like you are pushing me away now. It
wasn't the isolated lifestyle here that made her leave, Rand,
it was you.''

He raised his brows. ''Me?''

''Yes! You pretend that you don't need anybody. You
don't share anything on an emotional level. You make no
commitment to a relationship. That's what made Marina
leave. Not because of the hardships of ranch life in the Rift
Valley!''

''You dazzle me with your brilliant insights,'' he said
coldly.

''It's not so brilliant, Rand. It's easy to see. You're doing
the same thing to me.''

''And what am I doing, exactly?'' Stony, alien. She
wanted to beat his chest, break through that cold, angry bar-
rier, to find the love and softness inside. It was there, she
knew it was there because it would come out at unguarded
moments, like a shy, nocturnal animal afraid of the light. It
was there in his lovemaking, in the way he looked at her,
in the way he touched her.

''You *know* what you are doing, Rand.'' She closed her
eyes and suddenly her knees were shaking. ''If you really

want me to leave you, there is one way to make me leave of my own volition.''

She felt like she was standing at the edge of an abyss.

She had no choice, no choice at all.

She had to jump to save herself.

CHAPTER TWELVE

"AND what might that be?" Rand asked, his tone cool as if he was asking merely to be polite.

Her legs were trembling so hard, she had to sit down. She swallowed and for a moment she wasn't sure her voice would work.

"I'll leave if you look me straight in the eye and tell me that you don't love me."

He had never told her he loved her.

In the next moment her life could fall apart like a house of cards. All it would take was a certain few words from him. Simple words: *I don't love you.*

He stared at her for an endless, terrifying moment.

"I'm not playing games," he said stonily, and marched to the door.

Her heart was pounding against her rib cage. "Rand?"

He stopped, turned to look at her, eyes unreadable.

"I love you."

He just stood there, like a marble statue.

"I'm not leaving."

There was the longest silence.

"I never asked you to," he said, turned and was gone.

All the strength whooshed out of her as soon as he was out of sight. She sagged into a chair, pulled her knees up and curled into a ball and wept until she had no more tears left.

There was only one thing to do. Show him.

How she lived through the days and nights, she had no idea. The tension was terrible and she was exhausted from lack of sleep. She tried to tire herself by taking long walks in the morning. It didn't work. She lay next to him with only inches between them. Inches as big and barren as the Sahara Desert.

It was obvious Rand was sleeping restlessly as well and one night he was dreaming, muttering in his sleep. Words and sentence fragments she could not decipher. He was struggling with something, his body twisting and turning in the bed, the sounds coming from him tortured and agonized.

She reached out a hand and touched his arm, trying to calm him. He didn't even notice her touch. Moving closer, she whispered his name. He went on muttering.

She put her hand flat on his chest. "Rand, you're dreaming," she said softly. "Wake up."

His movements calmed, but he did not wake up. "Shanna?" he murmured.

"I'm here."

"But they were dancing." He turned his head back and forth, confusion in his voice.

"Who?"

"The Pokot, and the Turkana...all dressed up with their beads and feathers and spears to tell you goodbye."

"You were only dreaming."

"You didn't leave, then." It didn't sound as if he believed it. He was still half asleep.

She felt her throat close up. "No, I'm here," she whispered. "I'm not leaving." She shifted, lay against his side and put her cheek on his chest. "I'm here."

His heart was beating fast, his breathing ragged from imagined struggles. His hand touched her hair, slid down to her neck, her bare back. He sighed. His hand slipped down to her hip.

Feeling him touch her, feeling his body against her own made her flood with tenderness and love and heat.

He turned on his side, found her mouth with a groan and kissed her.

And kissed her. His mouth was eager and feverish, his hands hungry on her breasts, her belly. Breathless with an answering hunger, she kissed him back. His name escaped her on a moan, her body singing a delirious song of desire.

Maybe he was not able to share his soul with her in the daylight, but here, now, in the dark African night, they could share their passion and she could give him in the night what he wouldn't take in the day.

Only this. Only him. Only now.

It was wild and primal and urgent.

She could feel the desperation in the way he touched her, the force of his need. It swept her away in a turbulence of swirling, throbbing sensations.

It was hot and crazy and frenzied.

It was like it had never been before, like the sudden on-slaught of a summer storm, furious and passionate with thunder and lightning.

And then it was over.

Stillness. Darkness.

He held her close, their bodies damp and slippery, his breath hot against her skin.

"Shanna…" he murmured.

"I'm here," she said.

She fell into a deep, dreamless sleep.

The sound of something falling to the floor awoke her. A soft curse followed. She opened her eyes, seeing Rand getting dressed in the dark. Outside the world was full of morning noises but it was not yet light.

"What was that?" she asked.

"Nothing. I dropped my boot."

The night came back to her in a flash. His dreaming, their lovemaking.

"Rand?" she said softly.

"Go to sleep. It's early." His voice was matter-of-fact, devoid of softness, love. A chill settled in her chest.

She sat up and wiped the hair out of her face. "Rand, please...talk to me." She heard the pleading note in her own voice, let it trail away, afraid suddenly to go on, say all the other things in her mind. *Please tell me you love me. Please acknowledge what happened last night.*

He pulled on his other boot, not looking at her. "I've got to leave."

And he did, not coming over to kiss her goodbye, not even looking at her.

She lay back on the pillows and waited until she heard his car drive off. Then she got dressed and went for a walk.

With Rufus, the youngest of the dogs, by her side, she sat on a big rock, a favorite spot, and watched the baboons in the gorge. She'd forgotten to bring her binoculars, but she didn't care. She just sat there, thinking, seeing the antelope come for a drink at the pool below, hearing the chattering of the birds, seeing nothing at all. Her mind could only think of Rand, of what had happened last night.

Had he thought he'd been dreaming when they'd made love? Did he even remember it?

Rand did not make an appearance for lunch, but just after one, a dusty Land Cruiser drove up and a young girl got out, her strawberry-blond hair catching the sunlight. The driver of the vehicle disappeared in the direction of the servants' quarters.

Shanna happened to see the arrival from the sitting room and went to meet her, wondering who the girl could be. Wearing jeans and a short top, she hesitantly walked up to the house, looking around as if expecting something to jump at her at any moment. A plastic Kmart shopping bag dangled from her left hand.

"Hi," said Shanna.

The girl looked terrified. "Hi," she returned, her voice nervous. "I...I'd like to speak to Mr. Caldwell please, Rand Caldwell." She was beautiful with her pale reddish hair and green eyes. Frightened green eyes.

"He's not home right now."

"Oh." The girl seemed at a loss.

"Please, come in." She stuck out her hand. "I'm Shanna."

The girl took her hand. "I'm Holly Cooper. I...I don't want to disturb you."

"You're not."

As she moved through the living room toward the big doors that led to the veranda, she saw the girl gaze around her with curiosity.

"Oh," she said, "what an interesting house!"

"Yes, it is."

The veranda with its panoramic view made even more of an impression. For a moment she just stood there, looking in numb wonder.

"This is so awesome," she whispered.

"Yes. The veranda is my favorite place." Shanna gestured at one of the chairs. "Have a seat."

The girl hesitated and suddenly the fear was back in her face. "Is Rand's...Mr. Caldwell's father home?"

The question surprised Shanna. "No, he's not. He died several years ago."

Holly's eyes grew even wider and the stress seemed to rush out of her with an almost audible whoosh. "Oh, good," she said with such a sincere note of relief, Shanna couldn't help smiling.

The instant she heard herself say the words, the girl's body froze, and panic washed over her features. "Oh, I'm sorry! I'm so sorry! I didn't mean..."

Shanna touched her shoulder, gesturing her to sit down.

"I know," she said gently. "I know what you mean. It's all right."

Putting the plastic bag down, Holly sagged into a chair and buried her face in her hands. "I can't believe I said that," she moaned.

"Don't worry about it. I never met him and you didn't hurt my feelings or anything, okay? Now, can I get you a drink?"

The girl lifted her face and Shanna smiled at her, trying to ease the girl's discomfort.

"Please, yes, anything is fine," she said in a faint voice.

Catherine was already hovering at the door, and she asked her to bring two colas.

"So," she said, "is there anything I can help you with? Rand won't be back until dinnertime."

The girl bit her lip nervously. "Are you his wife?"

"No." What was she to say now? I live with him? I'm his girlfriend? His mistress in disfavor? Oh, please.

"Oh," said the girl. "You…live here?"

"Yes. I help out with the cooking, let's say."

Holly chuckled, her features relaxing. "I suppose I should tell you who I am."

"That would be nice," said Shanna with a smile.

Holly moistened her lips. She clasped her hands in her lap, twisting them like an awkward little girl.

"I'm his sister," she said.

"*Rand*'s sister?"

She nodded nervously. "Half sister, really. I…I don't think he knows."

"I don't understand," said Shanna, shaking her head. "Why wouldn't he know he has a sister?"

Holly swallowed. "He hasn't told you about his mother? No, I suppose not. He hates her." She winced. "It's so hard to understand, you know. I love my mother. I can't imagine why anyone would hate her." Tears swam in her eyes. "I'm sorry. I'm a wreck. I'm so glad you're here. I was so scared, but I had to do it. I had to come.''

''Why did you come?'' Shanna asked gently. Her heart went out to her. The girl looked brittle with nerves.

''I want to know my brother. I don't want anything from him, except to meet him. I mean, I have no other brothers and sisters and now that I know I have a brother...'' She swallowed. ''And I want it for my mother even more,'' she went on with a desperate note in her voice, as if she couldn't get the words out fast enough. ''She hasn't seen him since he was twelve. I didn't know any of it until two years ago, when my dad died, and it was so awful when she told me. She cried. I want to get the two together again. It's not right, you know, what happened. She loved him.''

Shanna sat very still and bits of conversation fluttered back into her mind, light as leaves floating in a breeze.

She was fun, Antonia had said. *We'd play the piano and we'd make up silly songs. Or she'd teach us how to dance.*

Gregarious, vivacious woman, Antonia's father had said.

''Where is your mother now?'' Shanna asked.

''In Nyahururu, at the Rhino Lodge. We arrived yesterday.''

Rand's mother was in Nyahururu. Shanna felt the strangest feeling, a lightness of expectation, of possibilities opening like flowers in the morning sun. It wasn't anything rational, she was aware of that. It could well spell disaster.

Holly took a deep breath, as if even speaking needed courage. ''I told her I'd go and see if I could meet Rand. I mean, he can't hate me, can he? He doesn't know me. He probably doesn't even know I exist. Has he ever mentioned me or my mother to you?''

Shanna shook her head. ''No. He doesn't talk much about his past.''

Holly bit her lip. ''Maybe it's not important to him.'' Her voice was low.

"Maybe it hurts too much," Shanna said softly.

The girl's eyes widened. "You think so?"

"It's very hard to know what he feels."

"Oh." She thought about that for a moment. "When do you expect him home?"

"Not until later tonight. Maybe it would be better if you'd go back to the Lodge and let me talk to him."

Relief flooded the girl's face. "Would you? Do you think he'll want to see me?"

"I don't know." And the terrible thing was that she really didn't know.

"My mother tried, you know. But they weren't happy together and he…" Her voice trailed away for a moment. "My mother became very depressed and Mr. Caldwell…he…hurt her very much and…" Clearly she had more to say about Rand's father but decided this might not be the right time. She glanced at her hands clenched in her lap. "She waited until Rand was twelve years old and then she left. She thought he would be old enough not to need her so much anymore, and she couldn't take him with her."

"Why not?"

"He belonged here, in Africa, she said. He was always out—hunting, fishing. She said it would be cruel to take him away from here, but that it was the most difficult thing she has ever done in her life. And then…" She swallowed again. "And then Rand's father wouldn't allow any contact so she never saw him again."

"It must have been very difficult for her." Her words sounded inadequate somehow, clichéd, but she couldn't think of what else to say.

Holly hesitated. "What's he like?" she asked then. "I mean, is he nice?" She looked embarrassed a little. "I guess you would think so."

"Not necessarily always, no," Shanna said dryly.

"My mom said he was quite wild as a boy, always out

running around in the bush, catching things, like snakes, and chameleons.'' She gave a little shiver and took a drink from her cola.

"He still tromps around in the bush, but generally speaking I'd say he's quite civilized now. He eats with a knife and fork and he's housebroken.''

Holly nearly choked on her drink, swallowing desperately. After this she was no longer nervous.

"Thank you for being so nice,'' she said when she got up to leave. "I hope you'll be able to…help out, I mean, so he'll want to see us.''

"I'll try.'' She had no idea how, but she would.

Holly hesitated for a moment. "Please try hard,'' she said softly. Then she bent down and picked up the plastic shopping bag next to her chair and handed it to her. "Would you give this to him? It's from my mother.''

Rand came home late, eating a warmed-up dinner in silence. Shanna left him to it, catching him afterward in the sitting room where he was rummaging through the book shelves looking for something, she didn't know what.

"Someone was here to see you this afternoon,'' she said, diving right in.

"Who? Why didn't you send him to the office?''

"I thought you were out since you didn't come home for lunch, and it's a her, not a him.''

"So, who was it?'' His back was still turned to her, his attention on the books in front of him.

Shanna didn't know how to tell him in any way that was not going to be a shock to him.

"Your sister,'' she said.

His hand stilled on the spine of a book. There was a silence and she could hear the throbbing of her own heart.

"I don't have a sister.''

"She's your mother's daughter, your half sister.''

He turned to face her. "What the hell is going on?" His voice was low with sudden anger, barely contained.

"Her name is Holly. She's eighteen and she came here because she wanted to meet her brother."

He stood rigidly still, his face unmoving and Shanna felt herself tremble at the thought of what his icy control was hiding.

"What did she want?"

"Just to meet you."

"Where is she now?"

"At the Lodge in Nyahururu." She swallowed. "Your mother is there, too. She wants to see you as well."

He cursed viciously. "I don't want to see them!"

"What are you afraid of?"

"I'm not afraid," he said contemptuously. "I have nothing to say to her. I was twelve years old and she left me. No letters, not even a wretched birthday card! Is she expecting me to open my arms and welcome her home?"

"I don't know, Rand, but why don't you find out? Why didn't you find out before? You studied in the States for a couple of years and you never made an attempt to find your mother? Weren't you curious? Didn't you want to know…"

"No, I didn't. If she wanted to see me, she knew where I was. She walked out on me and my father. She left us, not the other way around. It was her decision."

"Why did she leave?"

He gave a bitter little laugh. "She didn't like the life here. She wanted fun and excitement. We had parties here, and we went to other people's parties, but it wasn't enough. Eventually she took off with another man and never came back."

"Is that what your father told you?"

"That's the truth! And what the hell is this? This is none of your concern!"

It is my concern, because I love you, she wanted to say.

"There are always two sides to a story, you know, if not three or four. You were only twelve. Did it ever occur to you that maybe what you know is not the whole truth?"

"The whole truth?" he asked scathingly. "She was my *mother*. I *loved* her, and then she simply left one day. She didn't tell me until the night before. She promised to write, to have me come for visits to the States, holidays."

He had never said so much before and she didn't interrupt, afraid he might stop.

He turned away, as if he didn't want her to see his face. "I lay awake," he said tonelessly, "hoping there would be a letter the next day. Every day after class I would go to the school office and ask. For weeks on end, until I gave up. I didn't know where she was, how to contact her." He turned to face her again. "That's the truth I know."

She felt engulfed with pain, for him, for the boy he had been, the hopeless longing never fulfilled.

He rested his hands on the back of a chair and leaned toward her, looking hard into her eyes. "You know what I did?" he went on, as if suddenly he could no longer keep the words inside, as he had done for so long. "I made up scenarios in my head how the plane had crashed in the ocean so she was dead and that was the reason she did not write to me. It was easier to think she was dead than to know she had not kept her promise to me, that she had simply forgotten me."

"What about your father? What did he say?"

He straightened away from the chair and pushed his hands into his pockets. "The only thing he ever said was that she didn't belong on a ranch in Africa, that she had the morals of an alley cat, or something to that effect, and that we were better off without her. After that he never said another word about her. It was as if she had never existed for him. I asked and asked, and got nothing but silence."

"Don't you think you should hear your mother's side of the story?"

"After twenty-some years?" he asked bitterly. "Why the hell should I care now?"

"Because you do. And your sister does. She's a sweet girl, Rand, and she was a nervous wreck. I felt sorry for her." Shanna came to her feet. "She left something for you." She handed him the plastic shopping bag. For a moment she was afraid he did not want to take it, but he did. He reached in and took out a box, just a box that normally contained computer printer paper.

He stared at it. "What is this?" he said, his voice hoarse, as if afraid to know. He took the lid off the box, stared at the content, his face turning gray.

Shanna's heart began to pound as she looked at the pile of letters stacked neatly in the box, the one on top, clearly marked Return To Sender. Rand dropped the box on the coffee table, as if it were too heavy to hold on to. He sat down on the nearest seat, an ornately carved stool, and took out a letter.

She watched him, her heart pounding, then she turned and walked quietly out of the room.

Two endless hours later, she ventured back to the room and quietly opened the door. The table was strewn with cards, photographs, and handwritten sheets of paper. He still sat where she had left him, with both the dogs at his feet looking up at him with soulful, worried eyes. He was not reading now. Elbows on the table, he had his face buried in his hands, a picture of total despair. Her heart lurching, she rushed forward instinctively, stood behind him and put her arms around him, pressing herself against his back. She felt him dissolve, as if an iron control just melted away and he had no strength left. His body shuddered and a terrible strangled sound came from his throat, a buried agony erupting from its hiding place.

All she knew was to hold him, until his body calmed and silence filled the room. The only sounds came from outside, the incessant symphony of crickets and other insects setting the night air alive. For a while he did not move, stayed quiet in her embrace and a sweet gratitude filled her. He had not pushed her away.

Finally, slowly, he came to his feet.

"I have to think," he said tonelessly. He didn't look at her. He moved toward the French doors and stepped out into the night, like a sleepwalker. Rufus followed him out.

Fear leaped up inside her. "Rand!" she called.

"Go to bed, Shanna."

"It's night! You can't...please, don't go!"

He walked back inside, picked up his gun that stood by the door, and strode right back out. In that one instant she glimpsed his face and she knew she had to let him go and fight the demons of his soul alone.

Only she wished he didn't have to do it in an African night full of terrors.

CHAPTER THIRTEEN

SHE had never been so terrified in all her life. She sat by the dying fire, horrible scenarios growing wilder in her imagination by the minute. In her mind she pleaded with him to come back, but an hour passed and he didn't return. She went outside, stood on the front lawn and the *askari* came silently out of the shadows.

"He has not come back," she said to him in Swahili, as if he wouldn't have known. "Where did he go?"

"Don't worry, *memsab,*" he said kindly. "The *bwana* is skilled and clever, and he will come home safely. He has his *banduki,* and his dog."

What good was a gun if you couldn't see what jumped at you out of the darkness?

She was not to worry, the *askari* said again. Go to bed, go to sleep.

Right, she thought.

Back in the room, she could not sit still, could not get the terrible images out of her head, could not keep from hearing the sounds coming out of the darkness—the cough of a leopard, the whining of a pack of jackals. All the horror stories she had heard in the last few months crawled back into her consciousness, like poisonous spiders. Crazed with worry, her chest filled with clouds of cold fear, she paced the room, shivering.

She stared at the dead ashes in the fireplace, got down on her knees and built a new fire. She knew how to do that, had known it since she was a child, when her father had taught her. With a blanket wrapped around her, she sat on a chair and stared at the flames leaping and dancing around the wood.

At some point she must have dozed off from sheer exhaustion, because the roaring of lions awoke her with a start. Lions on the hunt.

It sounded terrifying in the night, too close for comfort. She raced to the door, outside and immediately out of nothing materialized the *askari*.

"*Memsab,* you must not worry. The *bwana* is safe. Go to sleep."

"The lions!" she said, her voice almost a shriek.

"The *simbas* are down in the gorge. The *bwana* would not go in the gorge in the night."

She went back inside, curled up in the chair like a child and wept. Come home, she pleaded silently. Please come home.

It was just before dawn when he finally walked through the door, Rufus at his heels. Relief at seeing him alive and well mingled with a rush of hot fury so sudden and intense, she could not contain it. She burst into a rage of tears. "How dare you do this to me!" she cried. "Walking off like that after dark…"

He stared at her blankly, as if he did not comprehend a word she said.

"What were you doing all night? Where were you?" High-pitched, her voice was filled with remembered terror.

"I was in the lookout at the water hole."

It was at least a mile away from the house, the trail leading through thick bushes and thorny trees full of dangerous shadows filled with unseen terrors.

He looked at her, still wearing her clothes, glanced at the dead fire, the blanket on the sofa. "I told you to go to sleep," he said wearily.

"Sleep? You thought I would *sleep?*"

"I'm sorry," he said, "I didn't mean for you to worry about me." He rubbed his neck. "I needed to be alone."

His face was haggard, his eyes full of torment.

Alone. The word touched something inside her. Alone fighting the ghosts from his past. The legacy from a mean-spirited old man who had taken from him his mother, his dreams, his innocence and faith in love.

His face was full of unspeakable sorrow, and the anger ebbed out of her. She wiped her face, but the tears kept flowing and she could no longer tell the reason—tears for him, for herself, for all the loss of love and hope he'd had as a boy, for all the fear in his heart that kept him from accepting her love, from believing it was real.

"Oh, Rand," she whispered, putting her heart in his name, and he reached out his hand to her, and she took it, feeling herself drawn into his arms, held safely against his chest.

"I'm sorry," he said again, and she heard an ocean of regret in his voice—for causing her worry, for all the times he had hurt her. "I'm sorry."

"I heard the lions," she said thickly. "I thought—"

"I was safe," he said quietly. "It's all right."

She didn't know how long they stood there, both exhausted, holding on to each other.

"Let's go to bed," he said, and they lay down with their clothes still on, holding on to each other, and slept.

The sun was full and hot in the sky when she awoke and she was alone in the bed. A note lay on his pillow, next to her head, where she would see it. *I love you. Don't leave,* she read.

The most beautiful words in the world.

She hugged the paper to her breast and cried.

It was after lunchtime before Rand came back. There was something different about him, his pace seemed easier, lighter, as if a dark heaviness had lifted from him.

"I went to see them," he said, putting his arms around her, holding her close.

"Are you okay?" she asked, her voice muffled against his chest.

"Yes, I'm okay."

For a moment they held each other silently. In the fever tree a single bird chirped a joyous song.

"I asked them to come stay with us," he said then. "They'll be here later this afternoon."

With us. How rich and wonderful those two words sounded to her. She smiled. "I thought, maybe, you'd bring them home with you right away."

He drew back and looked into her eyes. "I wanted to talk to you first."

"Okay." A nervous little shiver crept down her back. "How did it go, meeting them?"

"It was not easy, after twenty years." He pulled her down next to him on a cane bench in the shade, and he told her everything she had always wanted to know.

Told her about the grief and anger after his mother had left. About all the emotions that had wrenched themselves free when he had read the years of letters his mother had sent and that had never arrived.

"My father poisoned my life and I allowed him to," he said. "I should have gone looking for the answers myself when I grew older."

"He must have been a very unhappy man." She wondered what might have made him so, wondered why Rand's mother had married him, knowing she would probably never find out.

"Everything you said to me was true," he said finally. "I was too frightened to believe you would stay. I didn't want to go through it all again."

He paused, as if it were difficult to speak.

"You've heard about Marina. She was a...wonderful person, but I never allowed myself to love her, and in the end I drove her away. And I was driving you away. I know that now.''

She said little, just let him talk. He spoke for a very long time, his fear and grief finally set free from the prison of his anger.

''Why didn't you leave?'' he asked finally, taking her hand in his. ''After the way I treated you?''

''Because I love you and I know you love me, too. I knew it before I read your note this morning.''

''I never told you,'' he said softly, painfully.

''But I knew it anyway.''

''How?''

She smiled. ''Oh, Rand, how could I not know? You gave yourself away in all kinds of ways—the way you look at me sometimes, the way you make love to me. You just wouldn't say it out loud.''

''I wouldn't admit it to myself.''

''But I had decided I was going to make you acknowledge it, make you see it and say it. I just wasn't so sure how, but I was going to do it. And then fate gave me a little help.'' She grinned. ''If Holly hadn't shown up at the door today, who knows what I might have done.''

''You are very brave,'' he said. ''I think I said that once before.''

''Or just stubborn.''

He kissed her, then drew away to look into her eyes. ''I love you with all my heart. Will you please marry me?''

''Yes,'' she said, put her arms around his neck and kissed him with all the fervor and passion and love she could put into it, until finally, breathless, they drew apart.

''I have a question,'' Shanna said when she caught her breath.

''You always have questions,'' he said with faint humor in his voice.

She feigned a worried look. "What if your mother doesn't like me?"

For a fraction of a moment he looked stunned. Then he laughed. "My mother will love you," he said, drawing her back into his arms, holding her so tight she could hardly breathe.

And then the dogs began to bark and a Land Cruiser came rambling up the drive in a cloud of dust.

Rand's mother emerged from the car. She was tall and slim, with blond hair and green eyes—eyes that glanced around at the house, the garden, with an expression of such joy and bliss, it almost brought tears to Shanna's eyes.

The woman hugged Rand wordlessly, smiled warmly at Shanna and Shanna looked at her face and knew instantly that all these gossipy people had been right: Rand's mother was a lovely person.

Then Holly came flying across the lawn, wearing one shoe only. "My shoe! It's stuck under the seat!" She laughed, her hair flying around her face, nearly stumbling in her haste.

Gone was the terrified girl Shanna had met the day before. Holly ran up to Shanna and threw her arms around her.

"You did it!" she sang. "You did it!"

In bed, later that night, Rand held her very close and told her again that he loved her. That if she had left him…

She silenced him with her mouth.

"There's something else we need to talk about," he said a while later.

"Maybe it can wait until later," she whispered. "I don't feel like thinking a lot. I feel all warm and snuggly and cozy."

"You won't have to think about this. It's a warm and snuggly and cozy subject."

"Mmm," she said drowsily.

"I want us to have babies, any number you want."

She didn't feel drowsy anymore. "Oh, Rand," she whispered and felt her throat close. She swallowed. "I'll be happy to start with one."

"When? When do you want to start?"

His eagerness made her smile. "You told me you didn't see yourself as having children."

"Because I couldn't see myself with a wife." He stroked her face, his strong hand amazingly gentle. "Everything looks different now. I want to see you pregnant. I want us to have a baby. I want to see you holding it and loving it, knowing you're both mine."

"You really want to be a father?"

"Yes, I do." He said it so solemnly, it made her smile.

"I can see it clearly," he said. "You, me, kids."

Her heart overflowed with love. "Yes, right here in Paradise."

MILLS & BOON®

Makes any time special™

SEPTEMBER 2001 HARDBACK TITLES

ROMANCE™

Rafaello's Mistress *Lynne Graham*	H5476	0 263 17076 4
The Bellini Bride *Michelle Reid*	H5477	0 263 17077 2
Sleeping Partners *Helen Brooks*	H5478	0 263 17078 0
The Millionaire's Marriage *Catherine Spencer*		
	H5479	0 263 17079 9
Secretary on Demand *Cathy Williams*	H5480	0 263 17080 2
Wife in the Making *Lindsay Armstrong*	H5481	0 263 17081 0
The Italian Match *Kay Thorpe*	H5482	0 263 17082 9
Rand's Redemption *Karen van der Zee*	H5483	0 263 17083 7
Emma's Wedding *Betty Neels*	H5484	0 263 17084 5
Part-time Marriage *Jessica Steele*	H5485	0 263 17085 3
More Than A Millionaire *Sophie Weston*	H5486	0 263 17086 1
Bride on the Loose *Renee Roszel*	H5487	0 263 17087 X
Her Very Own Husband *Lauryn Chandler*	H5488	0 263 17088 8
His Wild Young Bride *Donna Clayton*	H5489	0 263 17089 6
Father in Secret *Fiona McArthur*	H5490	0 263 17090 X
Dr Carlisle's Child *Carol Marinelli*	H5491	0 263 17091 8

HISTORICAL ROMANCE™

Major Chancellor's Mission *Paula Marshall*	H511	0 263 16940 5
My Lady's Prisoner *Ann Elizabeth Cree*	H512	0 263 16941 3

MEDICAL ROMANCE™

Emergency Wedding *Marion Lennox*	M429	0 263 16916 2
A Nurse's Patience *Jessica Matthews*	M430	0 263 16917 0

MILLS & BOON®

Makes any time special™

SEPTEMBER 2001 LARGE PRINT TITLES

ROMANCE™

The Marriage Arrangement *Helen Bianchin*	1415	0 263 17228 7
Savage Innocence *Anne Mather*	1416	0 263 17229 5
A Convenient Husband *Kim Lawrence*	1417	0 263 17230 9
His Miracle Baby *Kate Walker*	1418	0 263 17231 7
Mistress on His Terms *Catherine Spencer*	1419	0 263 17232 5
Wife by Arrangement *Lucy Gordon*	1420	0 263 17233 3
Husband for a Year *Rebecca Winters*	1421	0 263 17234 1
An Independent Woman *Betty Neels*	1422	0 263 17235 X

HISTORICAL ROMANCE™

The Dollar Prince's Wife *Paula Marshall*	0 263 17192 2
A Penniless Prospect *Joanna Maitland*	0 263 17193 0

MEDICAL ROMANCE™

Doctor on Loan *Marion Lennox*	0 263 17140 X
A Nurse in Crisis *Lilian Darcy*	0 263 17141 8
Medic on Approval *Laura MacDonald*	0 263 17142 6
Touched by Angels *Jennifer Taylor*	0 263 17143 4

MILLS & BOON®

Makes any time special™

OCTOBER 2001 HARDBACK TITLES

ROMANCE™

The City-Girl Bride *Penny Jordan*	H5492	0 263 17092 6
The Husband Test *Helen Bianchin*	H5493	0 263 17093 4
The Italian's Runaway Bride *Jacqueline Baird*		
	H5494	0 263 17094 2
Legally His *Catherine George*	H5495	0 263 17095 0
Cole Cameron's Revenge *Sandra Marton*	H5496	0 263 17096 9
The Mistress Deal *Sandra Field*	H5497	0 263 17097 7
The Night of the Wedding *Kathryn Ross*	H5498	0 263 17098 5
Her Wealthy Husband *Margaret Mayo*	H5499	0 263 17099 3
Backwards Honeymoon *Leigh Michaels*	H5500	0 263 17100 0
Outback Fire *Margaret Way*	H5501	0 263 17101 9
Her Hired Husband *Renee Roszel*	H5502	0 263 17102 7
His Potential Wife *Grace Green*	H5503	0 263 17103 5
Stranded with a Tall, Dark Stranger *Laura Anthony*		
	H5504	0 263 17104 3
An Improbable Wife *Sally Carleen*	H5505	0 263 17105 1
A Christmas to Remember *Margaret Barker*		
	H5506	0 263 17106 X
The Doctor's Dilemma *Lucy Clark*	H5507	0 263 17107 8

HISTORICAL ROMANCE™

Wedding Night Revenge *Mary Brendan*	H513	0 263 16942 1
The Incomparable Countess *Mary Nichols*	H514	0 263 16943 X

MEDICAL ROMANCE™

The Perfect Christmas *Caroline Anderson*	M431	0 263 16918 9
Mistletoe Mother *Josie Metcalfe*	M432	0 263 16919 7

MILLS & BOON®

Makes any time special™

OCTOBER 2001 LARGE PRINT TITLES

ROMANCE™

A Perfect Night *Penny Jordan*	1423	0 263 17236 8
The Sweetest Revenge *Emma Darcy*	1424	0 263 17237 6
To Make a Marriage *Carole Mortimer*	1425	0 263 17238 4
The Boss's Secret Mistress *Alison Fraser*	1426	0 263 17239 2
Husband by Necessity *Lucy Gordon*	1427	0 263 17240 6
The Impetuous Bride *Caroline Anderson*	1428	0 263 17241 4
Twins Included! *Grace Green*	1429	0 263 17242 2
Their Baby Bargain *Marion Lennox*	1430	0 263 17243 0

HISTORICAL ROMANCE™

Lord Fox's Pleasure *Helen Dickson*	0 263 17194 9
A Trace of Memory *Elizabeth Bailey*	0 263 17195 7

MEDICAL ROMANCE™

Rescuing Dr Ryan *Caroline Anderson*	0 263 17144 2
Found: One Husband *Meredith Webber*	0 263 17145 0
A Wife for Dr Cunningham *Maggie Kingsley*	0 263 17146 9
Reluctant Partners *Margaret Barker*	0 263 17147 7